I0552561

SUGAR CRUSH

BLISS BAKERY SERIES

SUSAN SCOTT SHELLEY

Copyright © 2019 by Susan Scott Shelley

All rights reserved.

No part of this book may be reproduced in any form or by any electronic or mechanical means, including information storage and retrieval systems, without written permission from the author, except for the use of brief quotations in a book review.

Cover images used under license from Shutterstock and Canva Pro.

❀ Created with Vellum

CHAPTER ONE

Jack Kramer rubbed his hands over his face and then stared at the words filling his laptop screen. No doubt about it, this scene was the worst thing he'd ever written. Just like the rest of the book.

Low-grade panic pulsed with every heartbeat. His last horror novel had landed on every best-seller list and earned rave reviews. The expectations for this next book were high. So high. And six weeks to fix the book suddenly didn't seem like enough time. Hell, at this point, six *months* didn't seem like enough. But he'd never missed a deadline before, and wouldn't let himself start now. Inspiration *had* to strike.

Slamming the laptop closed, he scanned the tables of South Philadelphia's busiest diner. The clatter of dishes and hum of conversations, the scent of bacon and pancakes, the wait staff rushing around, and the customers enjoying their meals, he took it all in. People-watching and inventing stories for them had, at times, helped spark character and plot ideas. But nothing jumped out. Nothing at all.

Fresh frustration and desperation tangled together and pushed him to his feet.

As he stood, his friend Shane Brennan emerged like a beacon. Maybe not of inspiration, but of welcome and needed distraction.

Relief came as swiftly as the burst of hot air that accompanied Shane's entrance from the sun-soaked summer morning. Jack grinned and waved. "Hey. I didn't expect you for another half hour."

Dressed in a baseball cap, athletic shorts, and green T-shirt emblazoned with a bat and ball and logo of his family's gym, Shane set a duffel bag with a softball bat sticking out on the other side of the booth and slid in after it. "I need a favor."

Jack took one look at his oldest friend's face, the hopeful eyes, the winning smile, and the way his gaze darted to the bag that no doubt also held cleats and a mitt. "Ugh, no. Please don't ask me to do sports things."

Shane's smile faltered. "One of the guys on the softball team broke his leg rock climbing, so we're short one player. Can you fill in? It'll be for the rest of our season, the next four Sundays."

"The next *four*?" He gaped at the man. They'd been friends since high school. Eighteen years of memories should have been enough for Shane to know his idea wasn't the best. "Are you remembering my lack of athletic skills differently than I am?"

"Please? I called around, but no one else can do it. I need you." Shane shifted his attention to the waitress, who stopped by the table, holding two pots of coffee. "Regular, please. The strongest one you have."

She poured Shane's coffee and topped off Jack's. While she relayed the endless list of breakfast specials, Jack was hit with a flood of memories: Shane protecting him against school and neighborhood bullies all throughout high school.

Shane taking care of him the times he'd broken his leg and had been flattened by the flu. Shane being there for every failure and every success of Jack's writing career. Shane had always, *always* been there for him.

He placed his order and waited for Shane to do the same. The weight of guilt hung heavy. He owed Shane so much more than he could possibly ever repay. But doing something so far outside his comfort zone?

"I don't know, man. Watching a game is one thing, but actually playing one?" At thirty-two, memories of the taunts and torture he'd endured for his lack of knowledge about various games and his slow speed during gym classes and pickup games with neighborhood kids were still enough to keep him firmly on the sidelines. "I wouldn't be any good."

"You don't have to be good. We just need a body."

The words didn't make him feel any better. "Most people on a team would want someone who has some semblance of an idea about how to play."

Shane leaned across the table. "We're a really low-key team. It's more about having fun than winning."

"You say that now, but... What happens when I screw up?"

"One, you don't know for sure that you'll screw up." Shane held up a hand to cut off Jack's snorted protest. "And two, do you really think I'd put you in a situation where I'd let someone be awful to you?"

Still the protector. Jack had to smile. "No competitive jerks?"

"Not while I'm team captain." Shane's voice hardened, and determination edged over his features. "I'll put you in right field, or you can play catcher. And I'll make sure the rest of the team knows to help you out. You won't even have to play in the field every inning. And if you get on base, we have people acting as first and third base coaches, so they'll tell you what to do. The games aren't long. We play seven innings. It's maybe an hour or so."

Jack picked up his coffee, wrestling with uncertainty and insecurity. *Only an hour.* He could handle that, right? Besides, if Shane really needed him — and clearly, he did — then Jack couldn't let his best friend down. "All right. I guess it wouldn't suck too much. I'm in."

"Yes! Thank you." Shane grinned and lifted his own cup in a toast. "It'll be good for you. Fresh air, sunshine, exercise…"

"I get plenty of exercise at the gym." Working out at Shane's gym three to four times a week saw to that. The hours logged there helped to counteract the effects of sitting behind a desk for hours on end.

"I didn't see you there at all this week. Or last week."

"Yeah, well, I was busy trying to save my book." Glaring into his coffee, he slammed the cup down. Liquid splattered across the table and onto his computer. "Shit. Good thing it was closed."

Shane caught his wince as he mopped up the mess. "I'm guessing the book isn't going well?"

"It's a steaming hot pile of garbage." He tucked the laptop into his bag and stored it safely away. Before he could elaborate, the waitress arrived with their plates. His stomach growled at the scents and spread of eggs, toast, and bacon before him. Skipping meals when he was writing was a bad habit he needed to break. "The plot isn't working. The killer isn't coming to life on the page. And the rewrites are due in six weeks."

Steam from the coffee cup clouded Shane's sympathetic grimace. "I'm sorry. Anything I can do to help? We can bounce around ideas after the game."

"Thanks. I'll let you know." Brainstorming with his agent and his closest writer friends hadn't helped. Their suggestions had boxed him into a place where nothing felt right. The annoyance and worry over his train wreck of a book couldn't be pushed aside, and new worry over looking like an idiot at the softball game took over, wrapping around him like a boa constrictor squeezing the life out of its prey. He stabbed at his eggs. "Who's on the team, besides you and your brother Ryan?"

"There are twelve of us on the roster. Mostly people from the gym, so you've met almost all of them. And Ryan's friend Gabriel."

Jack's heartbeat stuttered. He jerked his head up. "Gabriel will be there?"

Shane's brows drew together. "That a problem?"

"No."

Yes. It was bad enough he'd be playing a game where he didn't know the finer points or anything beyond attempting to hit the ball and run around the bases. But to do that in front of Gabriel? Gabriel, with his light eyes and dark hair and sexy smile, who moved with such grace and strength? The moment he'd seen Gabriel at the Brennan family's holiday party six months earlier, he'd been struck by the man's stunning face and athletic build and the interest had only grown in their brief encounters since.

Shane raised a brow and then shrugged when Jack didn't elaborate and lifted a piece of bacon from his plate. "Anyway, he's played in a competitive rec league for years, but we convinced him to join us this season, now that he's working at Ashley's bakery. It might not be the family gym, but it's still a family business."

"Right." Jack nodded. He'd met Ashley several times since she and Shane's brother Xavier had gotten together through a charity baking competition. Thoughts drifting to how he'd run smack into Gabriel at the bakery's grand opening, and the man's quick reflexes that had saved him from crashing into the display case, Jack flushed with fresh embarrassment. Hopefully, Gabriel didn't think of him as an uncoordinated idiot. "Did she and Xavier set a date for the wedding yet?"

"Sometime next June, so almost a year away. Ryan and Everson are getting married on Valentine's Day, and they'll be sending out save the date cards soon, so maybe you could actually look through your mail and don't just assume it's all ads."

He'd *never* live that one down. "Dude. Just because I didn't see Leo and Kelsey's save the date card—"

"Or their actual invitation." Shane's reminder came with a raised brow and teasing smile.

"Okay, okay, I get it. At least I didn't miss their wedding or Everson and Ryan's engagement party in May." Jack ripped into his rye toast. He needed to change the subject before Shane could remember any of the other times Jack had missed out on things due to shutting out the world when lost in a story. "Your brothers all ended up with really good people."

"I know it." Shane's gaze shifted to the window and into the bright sunlight bathing the busy street. His voice held a hint of something Jack couldn't name. With a slight shake of his head, Shane turned back to his breakfast and loaded his fork with a combination of pancakes and sausage. "We'd better hurry up so we can get to the field in time for warm-ups. You're fine with what you're wearing. I have an extra mitt and a team T-shirt for you, and an old pair of cleats you can borrow. We need to stop somewhere and buy you a jock. Trust me, you don't want to risk not wearing a cup."

Nerves interfered with enjoying his breakfast, but Jack managed another swallow of toast. "I thought this wasn't a competitive league. I really need a jock?"

"You could still get hit by the ball, so yeah."

Jack winced. And then his thoughts flashed back to gym class and the kids who'd thought it was funny to throw a dodge ball or basketball at the faces of unsuspecting victims. Those jerks had inspired some of his earliest stories. "Maybe if I get hit in the head, inspiration for my book will strike."

It needed to strike too. And soon. But first, he needed to get through the horror of playing a softball game.

CHAPTER TWO

Bright sunlight baked the ball field.

Gabriel Spencer rushed across the grass and waved to the few teammates scattered around the bleachers and infield warming up for the game. He'd cut the arrival time closer than he'd liked, but the bakery had been slammed with customers. If it hadn't been for Ashley nudging him out of the shop, he'd have missed the start time for sure.

He set the bag holding his gear and the box from the bakery on the bench in the dugout. The muscles in his neck and shoulders protested his movements. After donning his cleats, he launched into a series of light stretches to ease the ache from a morning spent baking and decorating cupcakes and cookies.

To his right, his best friends Ryan and Austin tossed a softball back and forth. Joining their softball team had been the right move. With how busy life had gotten for all of them, the Sunday morning games guaranteed that he saw them at least once a week. He needed his squad, and the atmosphere was more relaxed and much happier than with his previous team.

Slipping his mitt in place, he flexed his hand in the well-worn leather and then jogged across dirt dotted with cleat marks to join them. "Did Shane find someone to fill in for Tanner?"

Ryan lobbed the ball cleanly to Austin. "Jack's going to fill in."

"Jack?" Gabriel gaped at Ryan as the ball left Austin's grip and arced in his direction. Instinct had him closing the mitt around the ball before it could fall to the grass.

"Shane's friend. You've met him."

Oh, yeah. They'd met. The most recent time — the bakery's grand opening — he'd nearly held Jack in his arms when they'd collided in the crowded room. His heart beat faster at the thought of the blond, dark-eyed, sexy writer. Spending the next hour or so within mere feet of the man who had captivated him since the first time they'd met at a Brennan family holiday gathering set off a swarm of butter-flies in his stomach. Willing them to settle, he fired the ball to Ryan. "I'm glad we won't have to forfeit."

"Me too." Ryan snagged the ball and tossed a grounder to Austin. "I love these games. It's a good team-building activity for the gym crew, and I get to see you guys. Hey, come over for dinner tonight. My dad and brothers will be there."

Austin sent Gabriel a grin and the ball. "An invite to family dinner? Does that mean your brothers annoying you with too much advice again?"

"I'm happy to step in and soak up the attention for you," Gabriel joked. But it was true. Not that he minded. He loved it. Being basically adopted as a part of the extended Brennan family was something really special. At twenty-seven, he'd finally found the family he'd needed his entire life.

Holding his hands up, Ryan shrugged and smiled. "Guilty. But really, Everson said to invite you." His face warmed as it always did when talking about his fiancé. "We wanted to try out the new grill. And since you guys bought it as our engagement present, it's only fair that you're there the first time we use it."

Ryan and Everson were so perfectly suited, it was like they'd been made specifically for each other. Happiness for his friend came with a side of envy. Gabriel kicked at a bald patch in the grass. He couldn't shake off the feeling fast enough. "Can I bring anything?"

"I've got it covered. Ashley said she'd bring something for dessert from the bakery, if there's anything left over."

"There might not be, with the way we've been selling out of stuff every day. I'll bake something just in case." He sent the ball to Ryan, rolled his shoulders, and did a mental rundown of the items in his pantry.

"Head's up!" Austin launched the ball.

Gabriel leaped for it, but it arced high and fast over his head. He watched its path until it disappeared from sight, then lowered his gaze to raise an eyebrow at his friend. "Really?"

Laughing at Austin's shrug, he spun and jogged across the field, scanning the grass for the ball. A flash of two figures wearing the team's green T-shirts captured his attention. Shane and Jack were walking toward him. Jack bent and scooped up the ball.

The butterflies in his stomach resumed their frantic beat. Gabriel slowed to a walk and then stopped a few feet in front of the men. The breeze carried the scent of coffee and bacon and something sweet. "Hey."

A worn baseball cap shielded Jack's face from the sun, but wisps of blond curls escaped at the sides. He smiled and held up the ball. "Hi. Here. We saw Austin's wild throw."

Gabriel lifted his mitt for Jack to toss the ball, but the man stepped closer and carefully placed it inside the glove. There wasn't any way his skin could feel the light contact from Jack's fingers through the worn leather, but Gabriel's pulse quickened just the same. He licked dry lips, and his gaze dropped from the deep brown eyes to the smile curling Jack's lips. Would that mouth feel as soft as it looked?

Shane clapped him on the back, shaking him from his musing. "Good to see you. Jack's going to join us today."

"Yeah. Ryan said." Heartbeat thumping as loud as a fastball slamming into a catcher's mitt, he extended his hand to Jack. "Thanks for filling in."

Jack's skin was firm and warm, his grip secure. His face creased with his wry smile. "You might not be thanking me once I'm out there."

Shaking his head, Shane led them toward the dugout. "I told you, you'll be fine."

The white-knuckled grip Jack had on his mitt as he surveyed the field suggested he didn't share that vision. "And you're a little too optimistic."

Gabriel walked by his side and wracked his brain for something to say. The few times they'd met at various Brennan family gatherings, there hadn't been much chance for a one-on-one conversation. He knew a lot less about the man than he wanted. "Have you played before?"

"Not in about fifteen years."

"It'll come back to you once you knock the rust off."

Jack stopped walking. He pushed up the cap's bill, and his wide-eyed, dark gaze darted from the field to the teammates gathering to their left, and back to Gabriel's face. A slight tremor shook his fingers as he jammed the cap back in place. "Picture your worst player, like someone who strikes out all the time and screws up every play, then exaggerate their mistakes by about a million. That's what you're getting with me. Seriously."

Surprise and sympathy swelled over the butterflies. He'd never have thought a man known for crafting the scariest stories would look genuinely afraid of playing a softball game. Gabriel fought the urge to lay a hand on Jack's shoulder. "Believe it or not, some of our players fall into that category, but it doesn't matter."

"Yeah, right." Shoulder rounding, Jack curled in on himself.

Gabriel couldn't resist any longer. He shifted closer and rested his hand on Jack's shoulder. The sun-warmed material scorched his palm, but he didn't let go. "We're the fun team in this league. The only rule we have is that no one is allowed to take the game too seriously."

Jack slowly let out a breath, and the tense muscles under Gabriel's hand eased. "Shane said that too. But, really?"

"Yeah. We like winning, of course, and we're lucky to have some pretty talented players, and we've been playing so well lately that we could make the playoffs if we keep it up. But the bottom line is having fun with your buddies." Reassuring words could only do so much. Jack needed to see the team in action and how they all helped and encouraged each other. Gabriel motioned him forward and started the introductions with the teammates closest to them.

Shane stood in the center of the crowd and clapped his hands together twice. "Okay, people, huddle up. Jack has nicely volunteered to fill in for Tanner. It's been a long time since he's played, so we all need to help him out today."

Gabriel nodded, gaze drawn once again to the brown eyes and planes and angles of Jack's face. Jack was at least five inches shorter than him, maybe five-foot-eight or five-nine. The T-shirt and athletic shorts showed off his lanky build. The few times he'd seen him, Jack had worn jeans and a sweater. *Jack the athlete* was a whole new fantasy... But for now, making sure that the man had a good time and felt supported on the field and in the dugout outweighed anything else.

"We'll rotate Jack between catcher and right field." Shane pointed as he continued issuing orders. "With four outfielders, two of you will be covering that side. Austin, you good with helping Jack out there?"

Austin tipped his baseball cap at Jack. "Sure."

"Me too." Chantel, one of the gym's personal trainers, adjusted her purple-streaked ponytail. "I'm pitching today. So if you're in as catcher, I'll cover home plate."

"Awesome. Here's the batting order." Shane held up a piece of paper. "No changes from last week. Jack will take Tanner's spot and bat seventh. Okay, everyone, let's go out there and have some fun."

As the team separated for final sips of water or uniform adjustments, and Shane went to talk to the umpire, Jack sat alone on the bench. A wave of protection surged over Gabriel. "If you have any questions about anything, let me know."

Jack nodded, face even paler than it had been moments earlier. "Shane gave me a crash course during our walk over here, but I'm sure I'll need help. Thanks."

"Remember, having fun is the most important thing."

"Right." Jack swallowed and nodded and he smiled, but his eyes still held doubt and worry.

When Shane returned, bat in hand, with Ryan in tow, Gabriel moved away. Jack didn't need him hovering while the Brennan brothers gave him any final pointers, but he stayed close enough to hopefully make Jack feel comfortable and to know that someone else had his back.

The first two innings passed quickly. Gabriel kept an eye on Jack when they were in the dugout and when on the field. Jack stuck close to Shane when he could, and kept quiet, but his eyes took in everything.

During the third inning, Jack went up to bat for the first time. From his tentative practice swings at the plate, his stance was too tense. Gabriel winced as Jack swung at the first pitch and missed.

Standing next to Gabe at the dugout's fence, Shane swore under his breath as another ball whizzed by Jack. "He looks like he's facing a firing squad." Then he called out, loud enough to be heard by their worried batter, "Good eye, Jack. Good eye!" The rest of the team joined in, shouting out their own encouragement.

Two painful pitches later, Jack struck out. Shoulders slumped, ears red, he entered the dugout. "Sorry, guys."

Shane clapped him on the back. "Don't worry about it. Seriously. Go grab some water and relax."

When Jack passed by, Gabe stopped him. "You looked good out there." At Jack's snort, he nodded. "No, really. A little tense, but your swing isn't bad at all." The man still didn't look convinced, so Gabe elaborated, "Even pro ball players fail to get on base about seventy percent of the time. And those are the All-Stars."

Jack's brows shot up. "Really?"

"Really." He led Jack farther into the dugout, grabbed the bakery box from the bench, and opened the lid to show sugar cookies iced in yellow and decorated with red to match the threading on a softball. *Nice Try*, *Home Run*, and other assorted encouragements were written across each one in green icing the same shade as the team's T-shirts. "Here, have a cookie. One of the perks of being on our team."

Jack gaped at him. "You give out *cookies*?"

"We're the fun team, remember? Of course, we give out cookies. Whether you strike out or knock in a home run, everyone deserves a little treat."

"But even if they strike out?" The raised brows and crinkled forehead spoke volumes.

Gabriel gestured for Jack to take one. "That's when they need them most."

Shane sauntered over and snagged a cookie with *All-Star* written on it. "The cookies were Gabe's idea. Everyone loves them. He makes them for every game."

The expression that lit across Jack's face was a cross between a smile and a smirk. He peered at Gabriel like he was an unknown creature that needed further study. "Careful, Shane. This guy might be trying to bribe people so he can take over as team captain."

"I wouldn't do that." Hurt and embarrassment swelled hotter than the sun's rays. Gabriel scowled and shut the lid. He couldn't tell whether Jack was kidding. He'd gotten that same look from his brothers too many times to count. It hadn't felt good then, and it didn't feel good now. Anger—at himself, at Jack—lit fast. He shoved the box into Shane's chest. "Ryan's at the plate. I'm up next."

As he walked away, Shane's voice followed him. "Jack, you'd better fix that as soon as he gets back here."

Shane in protector mode brought Gabriel's anger down a notch. He'd never had that support from his own brothers.

Ryan's line drive to left field earned him a double and got Chantel to third base. Gabe shouldered his bat, strode to home plate, took a few practice swings, and held steady at the first pitch.

"Ball!" The umpire's call was echoed by shouts of "Good eye!" by Gabe's teammates.

He adjusted his grip and his stance. Whatever Jack

thought of him or his cookies didn't matter. Whatever anyone thought of him wasn't his problem and shouldn't be his concern. Countless self-help books had told him that. Except... He *did* care what people thought. He cared too much. That was something he needed to work on.

In the corner of his vision, Jack and Shane leaned against the fence watching him. He needed to get a hit. Needed to show Jack that he was more than just some guy with questionable cookie-making motives. This team depended on him, and not just for the baked goods he brought with him.

He eyed the pitch, swung, and the ball connected with the bat with a loud metallic ping. It sailed deep into the outfield, landing on the grass right by the fence. Gabe took off for first base. He pumped his legs, rounded second, and nodded at the third base coach waving him on. He crossed home plate right after Ryan.

His friend caught him in a hug. "Dude! You almost knocked the ball clear out of the park. Nice firepower behind that swing today."

"Yeah, well, I had some unexpected motivation." He followed Ryan and Chantel into the dugout and exchanged high-fives with the team.

Jack stood at the end of the line and held out his hand. "Nice job."

"Thanks." Gabe allowed the high-five and then turned away.

"Wait." Jack stepped in front of him.

"What?"

"I'm sorry about what I said earlier. I was trying to joke around." Jack's dark gaze was direct, his voice solemn and sincere as he continued, "I swear."

Gabe caught Shane watching them from the other end of the dugout. Perhaps Jack was apologizing solely because of

Shane's urging. But as he studied Jack's face, the fire of anger faded to pale embers. "No worries."

"It's just…" Jack adjusted his cap and raised a brow. "I saw you helping out someone with their swing in the first inning, and then helping someone else fix their glove and then find a water bottle during the second. And then with the cookies… Well, you seem too nice to be real."

A lot of people seemed to be things that they weren't. He knew that all too well. But he'd been nothing but genuine with his friends and with this team. The flames of anger flared high and bright once again. "It's not an act."

"That's not what I—"

"Look, we're cool. Okay?" He blew out a breath. This wasn't the time or the place to dive into deep discussions, and he didn't want to share why Jack's words had touched a raw nerve. "Apology accepted."

Pasting on a smile, he turned his focus to the action on the ball field.

Thankfully, Austin struck out, ending the inning and the awkward conversation. Mitt in hand, Gabriel ran onto the field, found his spot in the infield, kicked the dirt, bounced on his toes, and readied himself as Chantel completed her warm-ups on the pitcher's mound.

The first batter got a single. The next one struck out. Gabriel kept glancing at Jack as the inning progressed. Kept reliving their conversation. Another batter struck out.

The next batter hit the ball in between right field and center field, giving the runner on first base time to advance to third on the play.

Behind home plate, Jack removed his hat and wiped his brow and then laughed at something the umpire said. His entire face lit up with that smile.

Gabriel sighed and turned his gaze skyward. Did the man

have to be so attractive? And why did Jack's opinion of him matter so much?

The ping of the ball connecting with the bat yanked his attention back to the field. The ball, a grounder, was coming right toward him. He scooped it up and turned toward first base, poised to throw the ball.

"No! Second! Second!" Ryan, from his position as first baseman, yelled waving for him to throw to second base instead.

Damn it.

Gabe spun toward second, but the runner who'd been on first was already almost there. The second baseman yelled, "Third's going home! Throw home! Throw home!"

Gabe turned again. The runner who'd been on third base was halfway to home plate. He gunned the ball. It sailed over Chantel and past Jack and slammed into the backstop.

The runner crossed home plate. The others were safe at first and second.

What should have been a routine double play had turned into a disaster because he was too busy stewing about Jack to think about the on-field situation before the ball was hit. He kicked the dirt, then raised his glove and acknowledged his teammates. "Sorry, guys."

No more thinking about anything that wasn't softball.

Throughout the rest of the game, he kept his attention on the field and on cheering for his teammates from the dugout. Two more hits for himself helped make up for his earlier mistake. He hadn't been able to completely banish Jack from his thoughts, but he hadn't screwed up anymore either. More importantly, the team got the win.

He sat in the dugout, switching out his cleats for sneakers

and listening to his teammates debate places to go to celebrate. A beer and a burger sounded good.

Jack approached him, hat in hand, and sat beside him. "For a writer, I haven't been great with words today. I'm sorry."

Gabe tossed his cleats into his bag. The game was over, his mood had shifted brighter thanks to the win and the sunshine and the time spent with his best friends. He didn't want any lingering issues with Jack. They only had three more games together anyway… unless the team made the playoffs. "Don't worry about it. You were nervous about playing."

"I was, but this was more than that." Brows raised, Jack bit his lip. "You distracted me."

A laugh huffed out as surprise shot through him. "Yeah? You distracted me too."

"From the moment I saw you today, and then with how nice you were to me, and everything else you did for everyone else. And making those cookies…" Jack glanced at the empty box, then he shifted closer to Gabe, leaned in, and lowered his voice. "I was distracted by an idea, by how perfect you'd be for my killer."

Killer? Gabe's gaze shot from where their thighs now touched to Jack's face. "Excuse me?"

"Your voice, your mannerisms, your happy cookies, how nice you've been to everyone…" Jack ticked each thing off on his fingers. "Hell, you even smell like cupcakes."

"I, ah, came right from the bakery."

"I've been watching you this whole game, and the image for the character is forming so clearly. You like working in the bakery?"

Confusion whirled as fast as a blender at high speed. Jack seemed to switch topics with every sentence he spoke. Was there a common thread? Gabriel blinked and focused on the last thing he'd said. "It's the best job in the world. I get to spend my time creating things that make people happy."

"But it's not all perfect all of the time, right?"

With his need for perfection, and the constant stream of customers, he worked non-stop, and the pressure was always on. "Busy and hectic a lot of the time, but Ashley's a great boss. I wouldn't want to do anything else."

Jack picked up Gabriel's mitt and ran his finger over the stitching. "You're obviously one of this team's star players. Have you ever starred in a book before?"

"Starred in a book?" He watched the long fingers stroke the leather, then dragged his gaze back to Jack's face. "What are you talking about?"

"The character inspiration I just mentioned. I want you to star in my novel. I wish I had something to write on or my laptop." Jack leaned down and retrieved his phone from Shane's bag. "This will work for now."

Gabe's brows drew together as Jack's fingers flew over the keypad. Anyone who knew him knew how much he *hated* horror and gore. The idea that he'd inspire something dark and sinister for one of Jack's books seemed almost laughable. Or terrifying. "But you said I was the inspiration for the *killer*. You really want to base a bad guy on me?"

Jack stopped typing. His gaze traveled over Gabriel's body, lingering on his face. "You're so perfect, you have no idea."

"Thanks, I guess." A rush of heat flooded his body, then his brain caught up with Jack's words. "I don't know what to say to that."

"Say you'll let me shadow you at the bakery. I need to spend some time learning more about you and what you do."

Having Jack there could potentially wreck his concentration, just as it had done on the ball field. There wasn't any room for error when it came to making customers' cake dreams come true. "I don't know. It's pretty busy, and…"

Shane joined them. "Jack, why do you want to shadow Gabe at the bakery?"

"Because he's the solution to my book nightmare."

"Yeah?" Shane grinned at Gabe and clapped Jack on the back. "That's great. I know how stressed you were. I'm glad Gabe can help you."

Gabriel swallowed and weakly smiled. Saying no to helping Jack might make the Brennans disappointed or angry with him. As Jack's best friend, Shane would surely be unhappy if Gabe turned him down. He couldn't allow that to happen, couldn't risk losing the support and brightness that Shane, Xavier, Ryan, and the rest of the family had brought to his life, no matter what. He depended on the security of knowing they were there for him for all of his highs and lows. "You'll still have to run things by Ashley. It's her bakery."

"She'll say yes. Here, I'll text her now." Shane pulled out his phone. While he typed, Gabriel turned back to Jack. Up close, he could see the lighter ring of caramel inside the dark chocolate irises. The gaze pulled him in and beckoned him to stay.

Jack beamed at him. All earlier traces of worry had disappeared. "This is saving me. I can't wait to get inside your head. When do you work next?"

"Tomorrow. Every day this week, actually." His face heated again as he caught Ryan and Austin watching them. Family dinner that night would be interesting.

Shane tucked his phone in his shorts pocket. "Ashley's on board. Jack, she said you can come in as much as you need."

"Great." Jack handed Gabriel his mitt and then held out his hand for a shake. "So, tomorrow then."

"Tomorrow." Their hands slid together. Gabriel's skin tingled at the touch, and a thrill raced through his blood. His fingers itched to prolong the contact, but he released his hold. If he'd inspired a romance novel hero, maybe he'd feel more confident. But a horror novel killer? He had no idea what to do with that, or what it said about him or Jack. "I can't wait."

CHAPTER THREE

Anticipation had kept sleep fitful, but Jack woke filled with energy. He rushed through his morning routine, unable to think about anything other than seeing Gabriel again. The fluttery feeling in his stomach spread throughout his body during his walk to the bakery, quickening his steps as his thoughts raced.

He slipped through Bliss Bakery's doors, and the scent of baked goodness enveloped him like a warm hug. He wove his way through the line of customers curling around the sunny shop and held his laptop bag closer to his body to avoid any possibility of knocking into anyone or anything.

Ashley waved to him from behind the register. "You can go on back."

He rounded the counter and hugged her. "Thanks for letting me be here."

"I'm happy to help. Let me know if you need anything. Gabe's two doors down the hall."

Nodding, he turned and nearly collided with a tall, slim man in a Bliss Bakery shirt carrying a tray of cupcakes. "Sorry."

"No worries." The man hoisted the tray higher and shifted out of the line of fire. "I'm Sebastian. You must be Jack."

Feeling the weight of all the customers' stares, Jack pressed himself against the wall. "I'll get out of your way."

Sebastian smiled and swept by him. In a fluid movement, he slid the tray into the display case and then moved behind the second register and waved over the next customer.

Jack backed into the hallway, thankful that the crisis had been averted. No way did he want to greet Gabriel wearing a shirt smashed with cake and frosting. Not to mention that he'd have ruined who knew how many hours worth of work the elaborately decorated cupcakes had taken.

As he approached the second door, his heart beat double-time. Nerves swelled and prickled. He glanced down at his T-shirt and jeans and the sneakers Gabe had suggested he wear for comfort and willed himself to not stumble into any other bakery employees or desserts.

The door was open. He paused in the threshold and stared inside.

Gabriel circled a table in the room's center, attention focused on a vivid purple cake. Worn jeans covered his long legs, and in the yellow T-shirt with Bliss Bakery's logo stamped across the front and back, he looked as edible as the sweet, fresh from the bakery, sugary goodness wafting Jack's way. With his strong, muscular body, he looked like he'd be more at home on a rugby field than in a bakery, and yet, with the piping bag in his hands and the way he bit his lip in concentration as he moved, Jack couldn't imagine him being anywhere else but the bakery.

With a soft knock, Jack stepped into the room. "Hi."

Gabriel lifted his head, and his blue eyes sparkled with his smile. His close-cropped beard was deadly sexy, and Jack's fingers itched to feel its softness. "You made it. Right on time."

The deep baritone sent a shiver up his spine. Jack glanced at the clock and then back at the streaks of purple frosting on Gabriel's apron. "We said to meet at ten, but you look like you've been here for a while."

"Since six o'clock."

Gaping at him, Jack set his bag on a stool. Stumbling to bed between three-thirty and four was his norm. "Six AM is like the middle of the night for me. Still, you could have had me meet you then."

"I thought we'd ease you into things. Today will be an overview of what we do and a tour of the space, and we're going to bake and decorate something. The next time you come in, you can arrive when I do. We'll open the store. Ashley is usually here first, but I've convinced her to let me open two days a week to give her a break."

"Cool. So, what's first?"

"You've seen the front where we sell everything. This room here is for decorating, and there's another for baking."

"Wait. Let me grab something for notes." He pulled a notebook and pen from his bag.

Gabriel took him around the large rooms, giving detailed explanations and descriptions of the ovens, the cooling racks, the machines and tools, the decorating stations, and the supplies. Then he showed Jack the walk-in freezer and fridge, a room that held various other supplies, a break room, and Ashley's office.

Jack jotted down page after page of information and little notes on Gabriel's mannerisms and the way his eyes lit up and the way he moved. Steady and patient, but something passionate simmered beneath that surface. He couldn't wait to dig it out.

Finally, Gabriel led him to a table in the decorating room where an entire tray of vanilla and chocolate cupcakes were decorated like a field of flowers. "I'll show you how to pipe a rose."

Quick, sure hands squeezed delicate, precise petals from a piping bag. In less than thirty seconds, a perfect pink rose in full bloom had formed. Jack moved in closer, sucking in a breath as his arm brushed the firm warmth of Gabriel's torso. "Can you do it again?"

Gabriel met his gaze, and the intensity sent a charge all the way to Jack's toes. "Sure. Slow and steady. With the wide part of the tip down and the narrow one up, angle it in and make a little cone." He worked as he spoke, and the bloom began to take shape. "Go around the outside edge and build it up to get a firm center. Then on the top, we're making the center of the rose by going in a circle and then bring that end down. Then make three petals, carefully turning the cupcake as you go. Start at the bottom and come up, and then back down. An up and down motion so that you don't see the beginning or the end of each petal. Make a second petal next to the first one, and then add a third. Stop to wipe off the pastry bag's tip, we want to keep that clean. Now, we'll make a row of five petals, just below this last one here. To make the rose fuller, we'll add another row of seven petals. Like this."

Jack watched, gaze fixed on the big hands slowly adding the delicate row of buttercream. Capable hands... He swallowed and forced his thoughts back to decorating.

Gabriel passed him the bag and a bare cupcake. "Try it."

"It's not going to look anything like yours." The bag was heavier than he'd expected. Jack adjusted his hold and mimicked Gabriel's movements as best he could in slow and careful squeezes. When he finished, his forearm ached, and the creation looked like a wilted, melted flower. "You can't sell that one."

"No, but we can eat it." With a wink and a smile, Gabe broke the cupcake in half and handed Jack the larger piece.

Strong notes of vanilla exploded on his tongue, and something else… "Is that bourbon?"

"Yeah. Like it?"

He nodded while he swallowed. "I have a pretty big sweet tooth. If I worked here, I think I'd be tempted to eat everything."

"I was like that at the first bakery I worked in, but after about a week of having basically unlimited access to cake, the temptation wore off."

"How did you get into baking?"

"I'm mostly self-taught. When I was a kid, a friend of mine had a mother who loved to bake. She let us help sometimes, and I thought it was really cool that you could take a handful of random ingredients and create a cake or a pie or cookies. My first job was working the counter at the corner bakery the summer I turned sixteen. I worked in a bakery through college, got a B.A. in English Literature—"

"No way. Me too." Jack saluted him with the remainder of his cupcake.

"Yeah?" Gabe's smile returned full-force, taking Jack's breath away. "I've always loved reading. I average about a book a week now. Maybe that can be character inspiration for your story?"

The image of Gabriel curled up in a chair, novel in hand, surrounded by stacks and stacks of books popped into his mind. Just when he'd thought it impossible for the man to become even more attractive… *Avid reader Gabriel* was a whole new fantasy. "I promise the killer will totally have a library at home."

"Good. I'm glad he'll have a redeeming quality."

"He'll have more than one. But for that, I need to get inside your head more. What do you like to read?"

"Biographies, fiction, science, cookbooks. I like things that make me laugh best, though." His expression grew serious. "I'm sorry I haven't read your books. I don't read horror. Blood and gore isn't my thing."

"That's all right. There are genres I don't read. I won't take it personally." He didn't. People liked what they liked. "I've never read a cookbook. Well, I mean, I *have* looked up recipes before. But I don't actually own a cookbook."

Gabriel's lips twitched. "No?"

"No." He made another note in his book. *Gabe's eyes crinkle when he smiles.* "How did you go from getting an English degree to being a full-time baker?"

"I originally wanted to teach. But I baked to relax and then started getting requests for cakes from friends. Baking things for people made them really happy, and I loved that feeling. Spending my days getting to do that fulfills something in me. Something that nothing else can." Gabe picked up the last bite of his cupcake. "Working here has been the best by far. Ashley's a great boss. She's open to collaborating and encourages Sebastian and me to share our ideas. It's a nice change from my last bakery. I owe Ryan a lot for suggesting me when Ashley needed to hire an assistant."

The Brennan brothers to the rescue once again. Jack smiled at the thought.

Gabriel dusted his hands and moved away from the table. "Break time's over. We're going to make a carrot cake. You can help grab ingredients."

That familiar rush of attraction stirred in Jack's blood as he followed the man into the baking room. "Shane said you're not from here originally."

"I moved here for school, then stayed. I'm from Ohio."

"Is your family still there? Tell me about them."

Gabriel stood still for a moment, holding bags of flour and sugar. Expression guarded, he placed the items on the counter. "What does that have to do with baking?"

Uh oh. The urge to delve deeper warred with the desire to smoothly change the subject. "They're a part of you. I'm looking for more character inspiration. Unless you don't want to talk about it."

"I'm not close to my family." Gabriel selected a bottle of vanilla from a shelf. "I have four brothers. I'm right in the middle."

"Classic middle child? I can work that into the character."

"Yeah, I guess I was. Still am, since I still don't like conflict." Shrugging, he continued, "My mom is a nurse. She worked the night shift for years, and my dad is a machine operator at a place that runs twenty-four seven. He was on second shift and still is, actually. So for a large part of my life, we kids kind of raised ourselves. Mom wanted quiet so she could sleep in the afternoon and evening before she went into work, and when I say quiet, I mean absolute silence in the house; otherwise, there was hell to pay. Dad worked four to midnight, so I barely saw him except for when he'd yell at us to get our asses out the door in the morning."

As the picture formed in his head of a young Gabriel amid that situation, Jack's heart squeezed for the man. "That's rough."

"It is what it is. A lot of people had it worse than I did." The way Gabriel had stiffened, the slight pinch of his mouth, the wounded expression in his gaze, suggested he'd had a rougher time than he wanted to admit.

He needed to get happy Gabe back. "Shane said you're renting Ryan's house."

"Shane seems to be saying a lot of things lately." But Gabriel smiled and nudged his shoulder into Jack's. "I moved into Ryan's old house a few months ago. This is actually the first time I've lived on my own. No roommates, no boyfriends."

He wasn't touching the boyfriend line, not at all. Shane had already told him Gabe was single, not that he'd tell Gabriel. "I like living alone. No one is there to get annoyed when I stay up all night writing. There isn't anyone there to compromise with or answer to or disappoint." The disappointment was the hardest to deal with. Experience was a cruel teacher. He was better off being alone. "There's a lot of freedom in it."

"There's a lot of loneliness too." Gabriel's words hung in the air, heavy and weary. Then he glanced at Jack, and the vulnerability in his gaze faded as determination took over. "But you're right, not having to constantly give in to keep the peace is a nice thing."

Jack followed him to the fridge. "Is that how it was with your brothers?"

"I really don't want to talk about my family anymore." He pulled out butter and cream cheese and handed them to Jack. "Set them down for me?"

"Sure. What do you want to talk about?"

"You." Gabriel pinned him in place with a stare that was part heated, part hungry. As Jack retreated, Gabe advanced, carrying eggs back to the counter. "Why horror?"

Jack placed the chilled items down. He'd shared his story with friends and readers many times, but telling it to Gabriel wasn't easy. "When I was in middle school, I was the shortest, skinniest kid in the class. I was clumsy and awkward and in advanced classes. I got bullied. A lot."

"I'm sorry that happened to you." Voice gentle, Gabriel

laid a hand on Jack's shoulder. "Kids can be jerks. Some of them never outgrow it."

He soaked in the warmth of the touch, and his nerves relaxed under that sympathetic gaze. "That's true. I started writing stories where horrible things would happen to the kids torturing me."

"I can see how that would be cathartic."

"It was." Jack toyed with the bottle of vanilla, spinning it in his hands. "And that's how I found horror. I liked writing, and I was good at it. I liked being able to completely control the world."

After a gentle squeeze, Gabriel removed his hand. He dumped the butter into a mixer. "My oldest brother was basically a bully to the rest of us. I never imagined anything bad happening to him, but when he ended up with poison ivy in some really inconvenient places one summer after he'd hidden my bike in the woods, I was pretty happy about that."

Jack snorted and set the bottle down. "He sounds like a jerk."

"He is. When I was six and he was ten, he told me that our parents had moved away because of me. I was a pretty trusting kid, so I fell for it. I was scared and upset, and then he's laughing at me. He was an asshole. The stories I could tell you…"

Sympathy and the desire to protect surged through him, and Jack placed a hand on Gabe's arm. "Want me to kill him off in the book?"

Gabriel opened his mouth, then closed it. His muscles flexed under Jack's hand. "I'd have to get back to you on that. I'm tempted to say yes, but I'm really not a violent person."

"More of a lover than a fighter?" Half-kidding, and not expecting a response, Jack lifted his hand. Heat flooded into him when Gabriel's hand came down over his, holding it in place.

"I guess you could say that." A small smile playing at his lips, Gabriel closed the distance between them. "You look more like a lover too. With your hair curling around your face, you remind me of an eighteenth century poet. Like Byron, or Shelley, or Keats."

Mouth gone dry, Jack licked his lips. Gabriel's gaze darted to his mouth, and Jack's heartbeat quickened. "I… You read much poetry?"

Gabriel tipped his head closer and leaned in like he was sharing a secret. "And the sunlight clasps the earth, and the moonbeams kiss the sea: what is all this sweet work worth, if thou kiss not me?"

Warmth flooded his body at the almost whispered words, the flames stoked higher by Gabriel's thumb tracing a pattern on his skin. "I'll take that quote from *Love's Philosophy* as a yes."

"What can I say? I have a soft spot for the romantic poets." The corners of his mouth lifted, and Gabriel raised his other hand to Jack's chest. He brushed at a smear of flour in slow, deliberate strokes as he held Jack's gaze.

Desire burned bright. Jack was more attracted to Gabriel than he'd been to anyone in ages. Character inspiration aside, the discoveries of the person beneath the handsome exterior were like gleaming gems, he wanted to keep digging and finding more.

Giving in to his earlier urge to touch Gabriel's beard, Jack cupped his cheek. It was as soft as he'd imagined. Slowly, he ran his finger over Gabriel's lips. Soft and warm, they parted the slightest bit. His blood sang with the temptation to go further and bring their mouths together, to push inside that wet heat and discover Gabriel's flavor. To feel that sculpted body pressed against his own. To indulge and savor the way that Gabriel's gaze demanded.

But voices carrying from the front room were a sharp reminder that they weren't alone.

Gabriel's gaze flicked to the door. He shook himself and covered Jack's hand and slowly drew it away from his face. "We, ah, have a cake to make."

"Right." Swallowing hard, Jack stepped back and straightened his shirt. Business, not pleasure.

But he wanted both.

CHAPTER FOUR

Gabriel checked his phone for messages as he walked to the bakery. Opening the shop with Jack was first on his agenda. At five minutes to six, the streets were relatively deserted, and the overcast sky made everything seem muted and sleepy.

Sleep hadn't come easily for him. He'd lain awake for hours, too excited about seeing Jack to properly settle down. And that wasn't good. A lack of sleep meant a lack of focus. There was too much to do today to allow for any mistakes. Adding Jack into the mix was a potential recipe for disaster. The writer was sweet and smart and attractive, and so very distracting.

They'd spent nearly all of Monday together, eight hours side by side, as Jack shadowed him. Another repeat lay ahead.

He rounded the corner. In the distance, a lone figure leaned against the bakery. As Gabe drew closer, Jack came into focus: eyes closed, head tilted back, blond curls blowing in the breeze, and hands tucked in his pockets. He wore the yellow Bliss Bakery T-shirt they'd given him on Monday, black jeans, and gray sneakers.

Sparks of attraction dotted along his skin, skittering up his spine. Gabe cleared his throat. "Jack?"

He startled and opened his eyes, blinked a few times, and then smiled. "Hi."

"Were you sleeping?"

"No." He rubbed his hands over his face. "Maybe. It's so early, it doesn't even seem real."

Chuckling, Gabe palmed his keys. "Come in. I'll get you some coffee."

"My hero." Jack pushed away from the wall and followed him inside.

Skin tingling from the awareness of Jack's presence, he typed in the code to silence the alarm and then worked his way through the shop, turning on lights. Rising extra early to open the shop didn't bother him. The peaceful moments spent alone without the hustle and bustle of a winding line of customers were a nice break. He could ease into baking and enjoy a cup of coffee amid a soothing silence.

The break room's coffee machine was calling his name. Filling it, he angled his head until he could see Jack. "So, the first thing I do is make coffee. While that's brewing, I set out the ingredients for the first bakes. We always have the same ten staples going, and then we'll have daily specials too."

Jack stifled a yawn. "What's first?"

"Blueberry and chocolate chip muffins." He moved into the baking room and began pulling out ingredients, murmuring his thanks as Jack took everything and set it on the counter. "After the muffins, we'll start the cupcakes. Sebastian will be here at seven, and he'll bake the cookies. And then we'll have everything ready when we open at eight o'clock."

For the next several minutes, he combined ingredients, explaining each step to Jack. The writer took notes in the leather-bound book he carried, dashing out line after line in even, black script.

Holding the tray level, he slid it into the first oven… which was cold. As were the two beside it. "Damn it."

"Problem?"

"I, um, forgot to preheat."

"Oh. That's important, right?"

"Right." Heat curled up his neck and into his cheeks and ears. He never forgot to preheat. Shaking his head, he flicked his gaze toward the ceiling. "And that's going to set us back now. On top of the regular items, we have to bake an order of one hundred cupcakes this morning. They're getting picked up at noon."

Jack pushed away from the counter and joined him. "What temperature do you need?"

"Three-fifty for the first two and three-seventy-five for the next four. I have it." As he spoke, he moved along the row of stainless steel, setting the temperatures. "You might as well grab your cup of coffee now. I'm going to start on the cupcakes, and hope I can get them into the ovens before the muffins are done. If I—" Turning, he bumped into Jack.

Jack stumbled two steps backward and into the table. He stifled another yawn, swaying, and leaned a hip on the table's edge, but overshot it and stumbled again.

Moving fast, Gabe grabbed hold of his shoulders and steadied him. "You're exhausted. Go home and go to bed."

"No, I'm doing this." Jack lifted his chin. The stubborn glint in his gaze was highlighted by the purple shadows framing the bottom half of his eyes. "I'll be fine. I've pulled all-nighters lots of times. I just need coffee. That full pot might be enough for a start."

"That's eight cups."

"Depends on the cup size. If I'm drinking out of the pot, it only counts as one."

"I don't think it works that way. If you pounded that much at once, you'd be buzzing all over the place."

A single brow lifted, and Jack's eyes gleamed. "Challenge accepted."

Despite himself, Gabe chuckled. And then realized that had probably been Jack's intention. He also realized he was still holding on to Jack's shoulders. They were warm and firm, and Gabe didn't want to let go. "Did you eat breakfast?"

"No, I…" Frowning, Jack raked a hand through his curls. "I ate a snack around midnight, and I went to bed at three. I woke up at five-thirty, got dressed and came right here."

"We have some actual food in the break room. Sebastian leaves fruit and boxes of cereal here. I have some granola bars. And there's leftover cake from yesterday. We were trying out a new recipe."

"Cake for breakfast? You really are my hero." The faint lines on his face deepened with his smile. Brown eyes danced as they held Gabe's gaze, and then Jack laid a hand on the center of Gabe's chest, over his heart. "Did you eat?"

The warmth seeping from Jack's hand spread out, heating his entire body. At that moment, he yearned to be an actual hero. Jack's hero. "Not yet. On days that I open, I usually grab something after I get the first bakes into the ovens."

One by one, the ovens beeped.

"Finally." He stepped back and hurried to the blueberry muffin trays. In the corner of his vision, Jack slid the two other trays with the chocolate chip muffins into the adjoining oven. "Thanks."

"Don't mention it. I'm going to grab some coffee. I'll bring you a cup."

Relief and gratitude mixed together, and Gabe smiled. "Now who's the hero?"

With a wink, Jack disappeared into the hall, and Gabe turned back to the ovens and set the timers, then double-checked the minutes were correct. He couldn't allow anymore mistakes. Onward to dealing with the cupcake recipes.

Focus, focus, focus.

They were recipes he made nearly every day, but he double-checked himself as he added ingredients. He couldn't afford to lose more time. Vanilla bourbon, then double chocolate, then lemon poppyseed. The strawberry lemonade was his favorite of the summer specials.

Footsteps, followed by the scent of coffee, announced Jack's return. He came in, carrying a tray with two mugs, creamer and sugar, two granola bars, and a big slice of cake. "I brought you breakfast."

"You can start eating. I'll take a quick break after I get these into the ovens." There was a minute left on the muffins. He moved fast, filling the cupcake tins.

Jack watched him for a moment, then picked up one of the scoops. "I'll do the chocolate ones."

Between supervising Jack and tending to his own trays, Gabe felt like his head was on a swivel. He stopped only to remove the muffins from the oven. Flavor by flavor, the cupcake trays were filled, and in tandem, Gabe and Jack got them all into the ovens.

Jack stretched his hands over his head, and his shirt rose, exposing a strip of his skin at his waistband. The barest rim of red stuck out from his jeans. Boxers or briefs, or maybe a combo? Before Gabe could wonder further, the shirt fell back in place, and Jack was grinning at him. "That was intense. I'm calling Shane later and telling him this counts as my arm workout for today."

"I'll vouch for you. Without your help, I'd still be three flavors behind."

"You can take a quick break now, right?"

His stomach grumbled. He pressed a hand over it and reached for one of the cups on the tray. "That coffee is calling my name."

"The granola bars are for you, too." Jack drained half a cup of coffee in two gulps. Then, with a wicked smile and dramatic raising of his fork, he tucked into the cake.

Nerves stirring, Gabe watched, waiting for his reaction. Would Jack like it?

Eyes closed, Jack withdrew the fork from his lips and moaned. The sound trailed over Gabe's skin like teasing fingers. It was all too easy to picture Jack in another, more intimate environment, moaning in pleasure for something other than a dessert.

"Like it?" His voice rasped, and the image of him and Jack together someplace dark and secluded continued to play in his mind.

"So good." Jack lifted another forkful and held it out. "Have some."

Even as Gabe leaned in, something told him to pull back, to remind himself that he was a professional and was *at work*, but he ignored that voice. Why listen to caution and reason when temptation was literally staring him in the face? Holding Jack's gaze, he reached for the fork. His hand closed over it, but Jack didn't let go. Together, they raised it to his lips. The chocolate was rich and complex and married quite nicely with the subtle notes of cherry. "I don't usually have cake for breakfast."

"It's good to be bad once in a while." Jack wagged his eyebrows and held up another forkful. The fingers on his other hand grazed Gabe's forearm, and his eyes were sleepy and seductive. "Come on, Gabriel. Be bad with me."

He couldn't resist. Threading his hand through Jack's curls, he leaned in and opened his mouth. Jack slowly slid the decadent bite inside. When he withdrew the fork, he brushed his finger over Gabe's lips. That contact sizzled through him, and Gabe swallowed the chocolate and then licked his lips, chasing Jack's flavor. "I should… get back to work. That special order of cupcakes isn't going to bake itself."

Jack watched him for a moment. He nodded and leaned back and grabbed one of the granola bars and ripped it open, then held it out to Gabe. "I'm slowing you down, aren't I? I'm sorry. I'll try to stay out of the way."

He accepted the bar and cast a rueful glance at the cupcakes baking in the ovens. "You weren't the one responsible for slowing things down today. You don't have to stay out of the way. I want you to get your hands dirty and learn how to do things and ask any questions you have. You want to get things right for the book. I hate when I'm reading something, and I can tell the author did zero research on a subject."

"I really appreciate you helping me. I realize now that in my excitement when I asked you at the game, I probably made it impossible for you to say no. I hope you're not mad." The contrite expression pulled at Gabe's sympathy.

"I'm happy to help you, Jack. I still don't know how I feel about being the inspiration for the killer, though." Wrapping his mind around that was still a bit of a trip. He broke off a piece of the granola bar. "But it is kind of cool. I mean, how many people can say they're the inspiration behind a book character?"

Jack's smile lit up his face. "The hero in my first

published novel is loosely based on Shane, but that's it for me so far. Until you."

"Wait. Shane gets to be a hero while I get to be the bad guy?"

Shrugging, Jack picked up his fork and loaded it with more cake. "In my opinion, the bad guys are always more interesting."

Bad guy. The term itself didn't bother him, but being cast as one certainly did. "Can I ask you something?"

"Sure."

"What about me says horror novel killer?"

Jack dropped his fork with a clatter and grasped Gabe's arm. "First, you're not the killer. This book isn't going to be *Gabriel Spencer, the deadly baker*. The aspects of your personality that I've seen, the sweetness, the happiness, the way you help everyone, I'm taking those bits and putting them into a character who needs something special, some things to redeem him, and also because all of those things will let him draw people in, unsuspecting."

"But I don't have a secret desire to end someone with a mixer or smother them with fondant." He squeezed one of the piping bags he'd set out too aggressively, and icing shot out, creating a splotch of red on the white circle of Jack's plate. Lips twitching with a smile, he met Jack's gaze.

"I believe you. You don't have those inclinations because you're not the killer. But you're giving me great ideas here. Smothered with fondant, brilliant." Laughing, he jotted a few lines into his notebook. His curls fell over his forehead, and Gabe's hand itched to draw them away from his face. "Maybe the character will have some of your mannerisms, and maybe he'll have brilliant blue eyes, dark hair, and be devastatingly handsome. He'll definitely have that sexy beard."

As much as the compliments thrilled him, they gave him a

new worry. How would things be if every time Jack saw Gabe, it was like the word *Killer* was flashing over his head? "Do you think you'll see him every time you see me?"

The smile left Jack's face. He set his notebook and pen aside, then stood and moved until he and Gabe were chest to chest. His hand was a warm weight on Gabe's shoulder. "I see *you,* Gabriel. Not some figment of my imagination. I promise I know the difference between fiction and reality."

The words soothed the worry. "Sometimes, I prefer fiction to real life, but in this case, I'm glad."

Jack's gaze journeyed over him from his eyes to his shoes and back again. "I'm glad too. You make a great fantasy, but an even better reality."

He made a great fantasy? Gabriel gaped at him. Something in his chest fluttered, and awareness buzzed along his skin. Mutual fantasizing, how about that?

Footsteps echoed from the hallway, and Sebastian's voice flowed over them. "Gabe?"

Was it already seven o'clock? He broke from Jack's magnetic gaze and called over his shoulder, "Baking room, buddy."

The warmth of Jack's hand slipped away, and he resumed his place at the table. "You should eat your granola bar, Gabe. Then we can start on those hundred cupcakes. Like you said, they aren't going to bake themselves."

"Right." He nodded and rolled his shoulders and pulled out the order slip. He had a job to do, and customers and Sebastian and Ashley counting on him.

No more distractions.

No matter how much Jack's presence pulled him in.

From his perch at the decorating room's large center table, Jack practiced piping roses and watched Sebastian pull sugar into a stunning display of abstract art in blues and purples. The man was talented and quiet, and after three days of working in his vicinity, Jack still didn't know anything personal about him.

Unlike Gabriel.

The hours together had given him a good look into the man. Mannerisms, work ethic, coffee preference, snippets of family background, his attention to detail, the way he made each customer smile… The list, written in extensive detail in his notebook, went on and on.

He and Gabe had spent the morning working the register. All of that *peopling* was more exhausting than all the hours spent on his feet in the kitchen.

The only thing he hadn't done during his three days at the bakery was take a custom order. He'd listened to Ashley take a few. And Gabe, from Jack's glance at the phone on the wall, was still involved in the one that had come in as they'd finished their time on the register. The red light was still lit, which meant that Gabe was still in Ashley's office, on the phone with a client who wanted to amend a cake order. Unless that call had ended and another had come in while Jack had been creating roses and playing with plot ideas. Either way, Gabe had been gone for a while. The roses were losing their appeal.

"Hey, Sebastian? Can I help you with anything?"

The pursed lips and doubtful expression were enough of an answer, but then Sebastian cocked his head and paused, and Jack could practically see the wheels turning. "I need to do a cake delivery. When I get back, I'll start on the sculptures for the children's summer reading program cake. I'm sure we can have you help out with that."

Jack's ears pricked, and his desire to help tripled. "Summer reading program?"

"It's held at the community center that's a few blocks away. Tonight is the kickoff party for their summer reading challenge. We're doing a large cake shaped like an open book, with all sorts of storybook characters popping out of it."

"That's awesome."

"I've been looking forward to making it all week. I know Gabe has too. I hope he finishes his call soon."

Footsteps echoed in the hallway. Gabe strode in, clutching a piece of paper. Lines fanned out from his eyes and creased his forehead. He jerked a hand through his hair and then pinched the bridge of his nose. "The wedding cake that needs to be delivered tonight by five o'clock? The one that we *finished*? The bride asked us to change the flowers. Instead of white roses on blue fondant, she now wants blue poppies cascading down the cake and white fondant, and still wants the intricate piping. And she wants to add on four two-layer cakes covered with purple hydrangeas to match the color of her bridesmaids' dresses."

Sebastian's brows shot up, he jerked his head back and gestured to the clock on the wall. "She's making changes now? The cake needs to be at the venue in four hours."

"Yep." Gabe's clipped tone matched the stiffness of his limbs as he paced from one end of the table to the other. "I stopped to see Ashley out front first. She called in reinforcements. Xavier and Mike are on their way in. They'll work the registers and handle the customers so the three of us can be back here."

Xavier was at the bakery as much as he could be outside of his football career. Their father was too. Every member of the Brennan family had helped out when needed. Jack appreciated the loyalty and dedication, especially since that assistance would help ease Gabe's current stress. When Gabe passed by again, Jack grabbed his arm to halt his strides, then moved behind him and began rubbing his shoulders. "What can I do to help?"

"You don't have to—"

"I know. But I want to." He dug his fingers into the muscles. So much tension stored there, like Gabe carried the weight of the world, or at least, the weight of the bakery. "So, put me where you want me."

Gabe turned his head, and the electricity in his gaze sent sparks through Jack. "If you really don't mind, can you wash some of the things in the sink?"

"I'll wash *all* of the things in the sink." He moved his massage to Gabe's neck. "Does this happen a lot?"

"This isn't the first time. People change their minds, especially when they've initially picked things to please people other than themselves, but this one wins for being the closest to the wedding start time."

Sebastian walked by, carrying his sugar masterpiece. "I'm taking the cake to the Art Museum. I should be back in forty-five minutes."

Feeling helpless, because only washing dishes seem like enough help, Jack stopped him. "Do you want me to drive it there, so you can stay here and do all the cake things with Gabe and Ashley?"

Sebastian glanced from Jack to Gabe to where Jack's hands laid on Gabe's shoulders. His eyes softened, and he smiled the biggest, most genuine smile Jack had seen from him all week. "As much as I would love that, I have to go. Gabe, don't worry, we'll get it done. Maybe call Ryan in too, he can help with the baking. Jack, just keep doing what you're doing."

Laughing, he thought of his attempts at the roses and his offer to help clean up. "Dish washer?"

"Morale booster and cheer squad." With that, Sebastian was gone.

Gabe leaned into Jack's hands. "Ryan's not a bad idea. He's helped out before. Sebastian had a bad cold a little while ago, and Ryan filled in for two days. I'll call him."

While Gabe was on his phone, Jack cleaned up the mess he'd left on the table. By the time he'd finished, Xavier and Mike's voices carried from the shop's front room. Jack presented his best-looking rose to Gabe. "What's the word on Ryan?"

"He's on his way." Gabe took the rose. "You're getting really good at these."

"You're just saying that to be nice."

"I am not. You—"

Ashley breezed in, looking as stressed as Gabe. "Help has arrived. The front lines are covered. I saw Sebastian drive away. By the time he gets back, we should be ready for him to work on molding the characters. Gabe, if you start carving the reading program cake, I'll start working on removing the roses and fondant from the wedding cake."

He nodded. "Ryan's on his way in. I thought, with the extra baking…"

"Good call." She rolled her shoulders and headed toward the walk-in refrigerator where the cakes were kept.

Gabriel turned until he and Jack faced each other. His blue eyes were still showing signs of strain, but the lines weren't as deep. "Thank you."

A brief massage wasn't much, but he would happily do whatever he could to help Gabe and the bakery succeed. "These hands are good for more than writing."

"I'm sure they're good at a lot of things." His hand met

the small of Jack's back. Fingers spread wide, it flexed once, as though he wanted to bring Jack closer, and then lowered to his side.

Ryan's voice, followed by too many footsteps for one person, broke the moment. "We're here."

"Who's we?"

Ryan and Austin trooped in. They both wore T-shirts with the family's gym logo, which meant they'd come straight from work. Austin bent and hugged Ashley. "I have an hour before my next training session, so I'm here to wash dishes or help clean up, whatever you need."

"Thank you both for coming in. I really need to hire some more people. It's been so busy."

"No worries, Ash." Ryan grabbed an apron off the hook by the door. "You have me for the rest of the afternoon. What kind of cakes am I baking?"

"I'll show you." She and Ryan fell into a conversation about the recipe as they walked away.

Left with Austin, Jack gestured to the sink. "You wash, and I'll dry?"

"Fine with me. How's it going here? How's your research?"

Picking up a towel, he launched into a description of the things he'd learned over the last week.

Gabriel started working at the table behind them. Wielding a knife, he carved off pieces of cake, sculpting the large rectangle into the shape of a book. He was like a sculptor with a piece of marble, except better, because *cake*. But Gabe, with the knife, gave him a solid idea for the book. He dropped the towel and opened his notebook.

When he returned to his duty, Austin had a pile of cleaned items waiting to be dried. Jack grabbed the first thing, a large bowl, and rubbed the towel over it, observing how Ryan and

Austin worked together to get Gabe to laugh and begin to relax. The bond between the three friends was obvious and reminded him of what he had with Shane.

Gabe completed the sculpting of the book and moved on to covering it with a sheet of fondant, an array of tools by his side. Ryan joined him and helped smooth it into place.

When Ryan moved to the other side of the room to help Ashley, Jack brought over a few recently dried items and slid into his vacated chair. "How's it going, Gabriel?"

He used one of the tools to create thin lines, giving the illusion of pages around the sides of the book. "Better now that we have help."

"What types of book characters will go on the cake?"

"Mostly ones from classic children's books. With a few more current ones the kids requested." Finally, *finally*, that smile came. "It should look pretty cool."

"The summer reading program got me thinking. Where you always a big reader, even as a kid?"

"Yeah. You?"

"Definitely. Both of my parents are, too. They were always giving me new books to try. They still do. I see them about once a year. They moved to Arizona years ago, but when I visit, I know there will be a stack of new books waiting in the guest room."

A line formed between Gabe's brows as he piped out lettering *Once upon a time…* "That sounds like heaven. On my last visit home, my older brother hid the book I'd brought with me, I guess, for old time's sake. I found it on my last day there. At least he hadn't ripped out any pages. He did that all the time when I was growing up. It got to the point that I had to start locking my books in the closet."

Anger burned, hot licks of flames, and the desire for vengeance merged with the urge to hug Gabriel in a pale attempt to make up for what he'd gone through. "*Please,* can I kill him off in the book?"

Lips pressed into a line, he set the piping bag down. "Well…"

"Gabe?" Ashley waved him over from her side of the room. "Can you help me with the flowers?"

"Sure."

As soon as Gabe walked away, Austin took his place and sat beside Jack. "Do it. Gabe's too nice to say yes to what you asked, but trust me, if you ever met his brother, you'd want to kill him off in your book within the first five minutes. If not for Gabe, do it for Ryan and me. We had to sit with that guy and his insults and backhanded compliments through a ball game a few years ago, and I was *this close* to knocking him out by the third inning. Ryan nearly did in the fifth. By the sixth inning, Gabe had enough, and we left. That was his last visit home."

"Sounds like it was pretty bad."

"It was. His dad's a miserable… well, let's just leave it at miserable, the kind of guy who isn't happy unless he's complaining about something. Gabe deserves better." Austin glanced at the doorway as Sebastian walked in. Their gazes collided and held, and then Sebastian ducked his head and strode to his work station with spots of color high in his cheeks. Austin continued to watch him, as still as a statue.

Jack nudged him and lowered his voice to a level that wouldn't carry farther than their side of the table. "What's going on there?"

The hulking personal trainer jerked toward him. "Unless you're prepared to answer the same question about Gabe, leave it alone."

"I…" Jack gaped at him, thoughts fuzzy, as a rush of adrenaline raced through his body. "I'll leave it alone."

Throughout the rest of the afternoon, and the frenzied rush to complete both cakes, Jack helped out where he could and mostly observed. He'd gathered enough notes to get started, likely enough to sustain him for the entire book. Knowing he was finished at the bakery and could again spend his days at home lost in his words should have filled him with happiness. But it didn't.

He wasn't ready to say goodbye to Gabriel. Not by even the smallest amount. And as the clock clicked toward closing time, he was running out of time to figure out what to do about it.

CHAPTER FIVE

Gabriel turned the *Closed* sign to face outward and locked the bakery's front door. Fridays were always busy, but today, with that last-minute cake order re-do, even more so. They'd completed every order, thanks to the extra help from Austin and the Brennans, and had sold out of everything in the display case. He'd been on his feet for hours. But quitting time was almost here.

Maybe he could risk asking Jack if he wanted to grab a drink or dinner. The writer had been at the bakery for three days, Monday, Wednesday, and Friday, and except for the brief lapse in judgment on Gabe's part Monday morning, and those few other lapses... things had remained strictly business.

Nearly kissing the man when his boss was only a few feet away? Where was his brain? Clearly not where it needed to be. The bright light of attraction had dimmed his common sense.

"Gabe?" Jack's voice came from behind him.

He turned and couldn't help smiling. Jack looked cute in his borrowed Bliss Bakery T-shirt. "Yeah?"

"I have all the notes I need to get started. Thank you for all of your help this week. I know I slowed you down some." Then he turned to Ashley and Sebastian. "Thanks for letting me hang out here and answering all my questions. I'll be sure to put you and the bakery in the book's acknowledgments, thanking you for the research opportunity. Life at Bliss can go back to normal now."

"You're done?" The words came out hoarse from Gabe's suddenly dry throat.

Jack patted his bag. "I think so." He'd helped open the store, had helped out at the front counter ringing up sales, and had helped in the creation of a few big cake orders. He'd even grown more competent at creating a buttercream rose.

"Oh." Drawn to Jack like the man was the sun in the sky, he should be happy that Jack wouldn't be there as a source of distraction any longer. But Jack's absence would be felt just as strongly. He wasn't ready to say goodbye.

He stood back as Jack hugged Ashley and shook Sebastian's hand, waiting as they joked around and did another round of *thanks* and *good lucks*.

Then Jack turned to him. "Ready to go?"

Surprised, Gabe almost turned around to make sure that Jack was speaking to him and not someone else. The other two days, they'd parted ways at the bakery. Blinking, Gabe glanced at Ashley. She nodded and waved him off. When he looked back at Jack, his heartbeat stuttered at Jack's smile. "Sure."

"Let's go."

Gabriel bid Sebastian and Ashley goodbye and walked out of the bakery with Jack into the hot, humid air blanketing the sidewalk. Nerves tingled along his skin, and his curiosity brewed. Whatever Jack had in mind, he was eager to follow.

Jack winced at the bright sun and slipped on his sunglasses.

Gabriel stopped and stared. "Did you just hiss at the sunlight?"

Slowly, Jack edged the glasses down and peered at Gabe from the tops. "Of course not."

"I swear I heard a hiss." He needed the laugh, needed something playful. His insides were wound too tight. If he didn't laugh, he'd probably do something stupid, like grab Jack and kiss him in full view of the bakery and anyone passing by. "You said you were a night owl. Aren't vampires called children of the night?"

That earned him a raised eyebrow. "I thought you didn't read horror novels."

"I don't. But I might have checked out your website. Do you really write at night, by candlelight with only the shadows as your muse?"

Jack laughed and shook his head. "It sounds good, doesn't it? But no, I don't. And I don't know any horror writer who fits the typical stereotype."

"No pet raven for you?"

Jack's head tilted back as he laughed again. "No. I might get a black cat someday though. I had one when I was a kid. Best cat ever. But back to my website bio, I actually do most of my writing at night. I'm definitely more of a night owl than early riser."

"And I'm the opposite. But I have to be at the bakery really early, so sleeping in isn't an option." All week, he'd answered Jack's questions about baking and decorating, and had tried to dodge the more personal questions, but hadn't gotten a chance to delve deeper into what made Jack tick. "So, where do you write? I'm trying to picture it."

Jack's lips pressed together for a moment. Gabe couldn't

see his eyes through the darkened shades but had zero doubt that he was being studied and measured. "You want to see where the magic happens?"

"I'd love to. I'm curious. I've never known a writer before." And he'd never wanted anyone the way he wanted Jack.

"Let's go. I'm about a fifteen-minute walk from here."

They turned right and headed down the block. The Brennan family's gym was on the corner. Gabe glanced in the windows as they passed by. Both Ryan and Shane were busy with people at the front desk. He looked at Jack. "I'm usually here four nights a week. I come after work."

"And I'm usually here around eleven or noon, right after I wake up. It's almost like we're two ships passing in the night."

Gabriel managed a smile for Jack, but the two ships thing brought his parents to mind. They were passing ships, passing over the breakfast table as they yelled about whose fault it was for whatever real or imagined infraction he or his brothers had committed as kids. He'd become an expert at walking on eggshells around them. Even now, the relationship was stilted, especially with his dad and oldest brother. For the millionth time, gratitude filled him for the open warmth of the Brennan family.

He glanced at Jack. "Austin and I helped Ryan and Everson address and put stamps on the save the date cards last night. I'm just realizing now that I could have hand-delivered yours to you today, instead of dropping it in the mail."

Jack grinned. "Thanks for reminding me. Same zip code, so it might have been delivered this afternoon. You can be my witness to Shane that I didn't just throw it out with the junk mail."

"Yeah, Ryan mentioned something about that last night."

Spots of red dotted Jack's cheeks. "What can I say? I unfortunately earned that reputation."

They chatted about the mutual Brennan brothers they knew for the rest of the walk.

Jack came to a stop outside of a modest brick row home. "We're here."

The house had a large front window with an empty flower box, and the shiny black front door had an ornate knocker. Jack unlocked the door and pushed it open. Sure enough, a few pieces of mail lay in the entry, with Ryan's card on top. Jack picked everything up and waved for Gabe to enter the darkened house first.

He spied a scary mask next to a skull on a shelf, and a sense of unease crept over his skin. He walked further into the living room, oddities catching his gaze from various places, and jumped when the front door slammed behind him. He spun around.

Jack frowned at the door as he locked it. "Sorry. It always does that on windy days. I tried to catch it, but got tangled up in my bag." He pulled the twisted strap off his arm and dropped the bag on the floor.

Right. Okay. Calm down.

Admonishing himself, Gabe turned and took in the room as light flooded it. Dark furniture filled the space. Dozens of horror movie collectibles—figurines, masks, and the like—adorned two massive bookshelves. Behind the memorabilia, books were crammed every which way onto the overburdened shelves. A row of DVDs on the shelf below the TV were all horror titles. Framed movie posters of classic horror films lined one of the light gray walls.

The living room opened to the kitchen, also a pale gray. Jack motioned for him to follow. "Can I get you a drink?"

"Coffee would be great." A shot of something stronger

would be better, but he hadn't eaten in several hours.

Jack set a mug with a cartoon version of the Crypt Keeper under the single-cup brewer and pressed a button. "I only have a dark roast blend."

"That's fine." Gabriel turned away from the mug as coffee began to gurgle and drip into the cup. That show had given him nightmares for weeks as a kid. His oldest brother had loved that series and seemed to take even more pleasure in it when he'd discovered just how much it had freaked Gabriel out. "How long have you lived here?"

"Almost seven years." He attached the save the date card to the fridge with a magnet of *The Scream* painting, then pulled out his phone and took a photo of it and grinned. "There. I'm sending Shane proof that I didn't lose this one."

"Even if you had lost it, I don't see Shane or Ryan letting you forget about the big day."

"Nope. Shane's already said he'll come over that morning and drag me out of bed if needed."

Gabriel had to bite his lip to prevent his own offer to come over and do the honors from spilling out.

Jack lifted the mug from the brewer and passed it over. "There's half and half in the fridge and sugar on the counter."

Gabriel turned the mug to the side showing the show's title. He opened the fridge. Besides the half and half, there was an orange, a bottle of wine, and a half-empty container of salsa. The temptation to offer to spring for dinner just to make sure the man had food was too strong to ignore. "Are you hungry? Because I'm starving. Want to split something? My treat."

Jack grinned as he held up his matching mug. "Great idea. There's a deli nearby that makes awesome roast beef sand-wiches. I have a stack of takeout menus in that top drawer."

"This drawer?" Gabe pulled it open. Instead of menus, the

drawer was filled with candy. Packs of Sour Patch Kids and Swedish fish mixed together with an assortment of individually wrapped hard candies, peanut butter cups, and chocolate kisses.

"Not that one. Never mind." Jack joined him. His cheeks had turned pink. "I told you I have a sweet tooth."

"There's nothing wrong with having a candy drawer."

"There might be more than a drawer." Jack pointed to two cabinets. "If you want cookies later, I have them all."

Gabe had to peek. Opening the doors revealed colorful boxes of cookies stacked in size order. Jack was right, he had every flavor and brand Gabe had ever seen. "Do you exist on sugar?"

"And coffee. It's writer fuel." Jack patted his mug. "I loved this show when I was a kid. Still do."

Gabriel hid his wrinkled nose behind his mug and took a long swallow. The coffee was rich, with just the right amount of sweetness. It would go perfectly with an indulgent dessert. The urge to bake something special, just for Jack, was overwhelming. "I make a dark chocolate cookie that has coffee in it. I'll bake you a batch. It could be good writer fuel."

Jack's brows lifted, and his eyes sparkled with his smile. "That's a sweet offer. Literally. But if you're doing that, I'll get the ingredients." His smile turned shy. "Maybe we could make them together."

"It's a date." An image formed so clearly of him and Jack in the kitchen, flour on their clothes and standing close together as they combined ingredients. Laughing and flirting. Touching. Maybe kissing. Maybe more. He shifted closer to Jack. "We could do it at my place. I have all the equipment."

Jack scanned his gaze over Gabe, from his eyes all the way down to his sneakers, then back up again. "I'm sure you do."

Heat flamed into Gabriel's body, and desire stoked the flames higher at the appreciative expression on Jack's face. He opened his mouth, unsure of how to respond, but Jack placed a finger over his lips.

"I hope I'm not assuming too much here. I like spending time with you, Gabriel. But I don't want to make you uncomfortable."

He covered Jack's hand with his and gently moved it away from his mouth, but didn't let go. Jack's hand felt too good and fit too well, resting in his larger grip. "I like spending time with you, too, Jack. And you're not assuming too much. Not by a long shot."

"Good. I wouldn't want to scare you off." Jack brought their joined hands to his lips and pressed a soft kiss on Gabriel's fingers in an almost courtly gesture.

Fully charmed, Gabriel smiled. "I'd love to cook you dinner that night too. You just have to let me know what you like."

"I'm not that picky. Despite the evidence, I don't eat candy or sweets for every meal. And I *can* cook." Jack winked and gave his hand a squeeze. He stepped back and waved toward the fridge and cabinets. "Convenience foods or take out often wins because it's just me, and I don't have the inclination to hang out in here for long periods of time." A single shoulder lifted in an elegant shrug, and he plucked a bag of candy from the drawer. "Let's order the sandwiches. And fries. They come with the best dipping sauce. You'll love it."

While Jack placed the order, Gabe studied the kitchen. An oven mitt on the end of the counter had scary clown faces all over it. Even the kitchen towels had bloody handprints embroidered in red thread. On the wall by the table, a clock hung with twelve eerie masks in the hour spots. And a toaster that imprinted a popular horror movie villain onto the pieces of toast sat next to the coffee brewer. Stifling a shudder, he turned back to Jack.

From Jack's side of the conversation, he knew the deli people by name, and they knew him well too. After setting aside his phone and murmuring that he needed to charge the thing, Jack picked up his coffee. "It'll be here in twenty minutes."

"That seems pretty fast."

"The deli owner is a fan. She gets advanced copies of my books, and I get fast sandwich delivery."

"That's a good system." Gabriel watched him over the rim of his mug. "We get repeat customers at the bakery, so that's sort of like a fan base."

"I'm so happy for Xavier and Ashley that it's going so well. Your bakery deserves every bit of praise and all the accolades. I've been really lucky. My readers have supported me from the beginning. I have a file saved with messages I've received from them over the years. It's a nice reminder on days when I'm worrying if my muse has left and if I'm still any good at this writing thing."

Gabe frowned as he thought of all of the accolades on Jack's website. That someone so successful could be riddled with such doubt surprised him. "You're a multiple bestseller. You've won a lot of awards."

"Doesn't matter. I still have days where I feel like a hack." Jack set his mug down and then laid his hand on Gabriel's shoulder. "And I was ripping my hair out over this book being a dead end, but thanks to you, my energy is flowing."

He placed his coffee next to Jack's, savoring having the man so close to him, and gave in to the temptation to brush his fingers through the curls hanging near Jack's face. They were standing so close, a simple shift of the hips would bring them almost into each other's arms. "I'm glad. Your hair is too nice to be ripped out."

Spots of color bloomed in Jack's cheeks with his soft smile. He ran a hand down Gabe's arm. "Let me show you the office."

Gabe fought off goosebumps and followed him, his gaze on Jack as they climbed the steps to the second floor. The office was across the hall from the top of the stairs and continued the Ode to Horror theme from the lower level. Every surface and corner from the desk to the filing cabinet to the shelves against the wall contained creepy elements.

"You have a lot of horror stuff."

"I've been collecting it for years. Let me give you the rest of the tour."

The bathroom had a shower curtain with a large image of a man wielding a bloody knife and a white bath mat with red spatters and footprints. A chill skated up Gabe's spine. He couldn't imagine living in a house like this. The small guest bedroom and Jack's master bedroom had a mixture of horror-related artwork and prints of iconic Philadelphia landmarks on the walls.

Turning away from a watercolor of Boathouse Row, Gabe spied a stack of horror novels on a small bookshelf near Jack's bed. The gory cover of the top book was almost enough to ruin his appetite.

Maybe he and Jack were too different. The chemistry was real and palpable, but their tastes were pretty far apart. How much would that matter?

He turned to leave, but Jack's hand on his arm stopped him. "Wait. I want to show you something."

Jack rifled through the stack of books. Frowning, he

crouched and looked under the bed, then stood and pulled back the bedspread.

Thoughts of tangling with Jack on the dark sheets tightened his jeans. Gabe discreetly adjusted himself.

"There it is." Jack pulled a book from beneath his pillow. "I found this in the downstairs bookshelf last night. I fell asleep reading it and thinking of you."

Gabriel's hands closed over the anthology of English romantic poetry. His breath caught, and his heartbeat quickened at the desire burning in Jack's eyes. "Did you?"

"*Love's Philosophy* is in there. When I read it, I pictured your voice saying the words." Jack's voice, soft like sharing a secret, gave life to Gabe's new fantasy: He and Jack, in bed, whispering the words against each other's skin.

The doorbell chimed, startling him.

Jack cleared his throat. "Food's probably here."

"Right. We should go down." But his feet felt rooted to the spot and didn't want to break the magic of the moment by moving even an inch.

Jack shifted closer. He ran his hand down Gabriel's arm. "Maybe you'll read some tonight and think of me."

"What makes you think I haven't already?" Gabe set the book on top of the pile. Sounds of knocking accompanied another chime of the doorbell. He forced himself to break the connection with Jack and move to the door. They trooped downstairs, and he pushed money into the delivery guy's hand before Jack could pull out his wallet, then waved off Jack's protests. "Ordering was my idea, remember?"

Arms full of the food, Jack bumped the door closed with his hip. "But I'm the one who invited you over. Dinner's on me next time. Maybe every time. We can call it an incentive for helping with my book character's development."

He rescued one of the bags before it could fall to the floor and followed Jack into the kitchen. "I thought you might be finished with that part because you said you were done at the bakery."

After depositing the bags on the table, Jack met his gaze. "I still need you."

The words relieved him on a level he hadn't expected. "I'm glad."

"Yeah?" Brows raised, Jack bit his lip and ran a hand through his hair. "I didn't annoy you too much this week?"

"Annoy? Definitely not." Only a few steps separated them. Gabriel eliminated the distance. "Distract? Definitely yes."

Jack's lips parted with his soft inhale. His tongue peeked out to wet his lips, and he looked up at Gabe, eyes shining, and shifted even closer. "The feeling's mutual."

"I distract you?" The idea was gratifying.

"So much." Voice soft, Jack stroked warm fingers along Gabe's beard. Their faces were inches apart. "All week, I was distracted by how much I want to kiss you."

Desire pounded a steady beat, demanding action. Gabriel clasped Jack's shoulders and then flexed his hands, kneading the muscles, aching to get closer. "Like you just said, the feeling's mutual."

"So maybe we should stop thinking about it and just… act." Jack slid his hand into Gabe's hair. He strained forward, and Gabe pulled him the rest of the way.

The first touch of soft lips robbed him of his breath and shot electricity through him. It was like nothing he'd felt before. Soft and hot, and *Jack*. The sweetness from the candy lingered among the darker notes from the coffee. *Addicting*. And he needed more. Clutching fistfuls of Jack's hair, he angled their heads until he could deepen the kiss.

Jack met him head-on, licking at Gabe's mouth, seeking

entry, fighting for control as they tangled together, torso to torso, and tasted and tempted and teased. That wicked tongue sent tingles all the way to Gabe's dick. Pulse throbbing with *want, want, want,* he gave in, letting Jack take the lead.

Strong hands backed him into the counter, and then Jack pressed in, keeping him there, eliminating every inch of space between them. He moaned as Jack's hands roamed to his chest, raking over the material, then traced his lips along Jack's jawline, eliciting a shiver from the sexy writer. Jack directed Gabriel's mouth back to his own and kissed him as though Gabe was the source of everything necessary in life, as vital as air and water and sunlight.

To Gabriel, Jack was as bright as the sun.

Kissing Jack was everything he'd dreamed it would be.

When breathing became necessary, he pulled back and stared into Jack's deep chocolate eyes. His own stunned expression reflected back to him.

Jack gazed at him, lips swollen and red and slightly parted. "Thinking about what just happened will be a whole other distraction."

One he already wanted to do again. But Gabriel forced himself to lighten his hold. His stomach was grumbling, so was Jack's, and their quick break for lunch at the bakery had been too many hours ago. He smoothed Jack's hair and then his shirt while Jack did the same to him, warm hands stirring up the craving for *more* all over again. "We should eat dinner."

"Right." With a firm nod, Jack stepped back.

They divided the food and sat side-by-side at the table. He listened to Jack's ratings for all the take out places and diners in the neighborhood and had Jack laughing over stories of the time he, Ryan, and Austin had rented a house at the shore for the week where everything that could have gone wrong, did.

When he glanced at the microwave's clock, he blinked at the time. Two hours had passed since they'd sat down.

Gathering the trash, he stood. He wasn't ready to say goodnight to Jack. "I'm meeting Ryan, Everson, and Austin to watch the ball game. Want to come?"

Jack looked at the time, and his brows shot up. "I need to get to work. I have a lot of writing to do."

"I understand." He threw out the trash, wishing he could toss his disappointment as easily. "I'll see you on Sunday at the game."

"Could we could meet earlier, just the two of us? Maybe you could help me with batting? I want to be better than I was last time. I hate the idea of letting Shane and the team down."

"You're not letting anyone down. You showed up, didn't you?"

"It would be nice to not strike out every at-bat."

"I'll help you." Giving in to the urge to touch, he rested his hands on Jack's waist. "It's all in the hips."

Jack smiled at him and brought his hands to Gabe's chest. "I like these lessons already."

With Jack's lips so close, he delved in for another taste. His nerve endings stirred, tingling through his entire body as Jack's arms came around him and held tight, prolonging the kisses with more of his own.

Long moments later, he made himself draw back, bid Jack goodnight, and left.

His thoughts stayed on Jack for the rest of the evening.

Giving in to this attraction… He and Jack hardly had anything in common, but the connection felt too strong to ignore.

He wasn't sure what to do about it. All he knew was that he wanted more.

CHAPTER SIX

Jack arrived at the softball field at ten-thirty, a full hour before the game. In contrast to the previous week, no shouts of laughter carried on the wind. There weren't people playing catch or taking practice swings. There wasn't anyone at all.

The overcast sky held the warning of a storm. The air seemed charged with extra energy. The heavy anticipation of *something* was everywhere.

Except…

Maybe it was all only him projecting his eagerness to see Gabriel again. Inviting Gabe into his home, his private space, his safe nest from the world, had been a whim, but he'd enjoyed every minute of it. Especially those kisses. All of Friday night and Saturday while he worked, his thoughts had kept drifting back to the few hours they'd spent together.

Gabriel entered the field from the opposite side and waved to him, then disappeared into the dugout. Jack quickened his pace. Given how they'd left things, could he kiss Gabriel hello? Should he go for a handshake instead? Or nothing at all?

When he entered the dugout, Gabe was tying the laces of

his cleats. He looked up and dazzled Jack with his smile. "Hey."

"Hi." Careful not to disturb the bakery box, he set his bag beside Gabe's on the bench, then changed into his cleats. "I figured we'd have some privacy by getting here so early, but I didn't expect the field to be deserted."

"Ours is the first game on today's schedule. Plus, I think the threat of rain might be keeping some people away." He peered at the sky. "I hope the storm holds off until after the game."

"Me too. I don't want to play in a downpour. I have a hard enough time figuring out what's going on, I don't need a sheet of rain obscuring my vision."

Laughing, Gabriel rose and extended his hand to Jack, and pulled him to standing. Then, he leaned in and brushed their lips together in a feather-light kiss. "Come on. Let's work on your stance."

Lips buzzing from the light touch, Jack stepped up to home plate and got into position, bat resting on his shoulder. Then he swung the bat as he had in the previous game. "Well?"

"Your swing is good, but your hips and legs need adjusting. And you're standing too close to the plate." Gabriel joined him and motioned for Jack to give him the bat. "Watch me. You want to put more weight on your back leg. And when you start to swing, let the movement come from your hips. That's where the power is. And then bring your arms across your body like you were doing. But you stopped too soon. You need to follow through more."

Gabe demonstrated twice more, then handed off the bat.

Jack planted his feet where Gabriel had been, got into position, and then swung, following through with his body. "How was that?"

"Better." Gabriel stepped behind Jack, and his hands clamped on Jack's hips. "Remember, load your weight onto this leg." He patted Jack's right thigh. "And then when you swing, you're going to lead with your hips." His hands touched Jack's hips once again, guiding the movement. "And then step into it with your left leg." A small tap followed on Jack's outer left thigh. "It'll give you more power."

The wind danced around them, stirring up the *fresh from the bakery* scent. Jack glanced over his shoulder and met Gabe's gaze. "Maybe you could help me like this during each of my at-bats today."

"I think the umpire and the other team might have a problem with that." Gabriel slid his hands around Jack's stomach and drew him tight against his chest. "But I like being here."

Jack leaned back and threaded his fingers through Gabriel's hair. With Gabe's arms wrapped around him so strong, he shivered at the delicious combination of desire and security.

Gabriel's beard brushed Jack's neck, and then he mouthed kisses along the side. Jack groaned as goosebumps rose and angled his head to give Gabe better access.

He would happily tug Gabe to the ground and roll around to get the scent and the feel of Gabriel all over his body. His groin tightened, his body tingled, and he groaned again when his cup became painfully uncomfortable. "We should get back to batting."

"Right." Gabriel pressed a final kiss to his neck then pulled away. "Sorry, I got a little distracted."

Jack gave up discreetly trying to adjust his cup. "I'm not stopping because I want to."

"Hey, same boat over here." Gabriel tugged an unsteady hand through his hair. "I've been reciting the stats of the

Phillies World Series team for the last few minutes to try staying in control."

They shared a smile. Then Jack remembered the bat in his hand. "Is there anything else I can work on?"

"I'll pitch a few balls to you. Going to the batting cages a few times wouldn't be a bad idea either. Honestly, everyone's stance is going to be a little bit different. The most important thing is that you're comfortable up there at the plate."

For the next twenty minutes, Gabe patiently pitched the ball. The first time Jack made contact with the ball, the ping off the bat was followed by a stinging sensation in his hands. He shook it off, wincing. By the fifth time, he swore a string of expletives and dropped the bat. If getting a hit hurt this much, he'd gladly keep his undefeated strikeout record.

Gabe trotted to his side. "Try to focus on hitting the ball with the barrel of the bat and not so close to your hands. The closer to your hands, the more the chance of it vibrating and hurting you."

"I think you're overestimating my abilities as a softball player. I'm just lucky if I manage to hit the ball at all."

After rescuing the bat, Gabriel slipped an arm around Jack's waist. "Come on, let's take a break. We've done enough for today."

He walked with Gabe back to the dugout. The water bottle he'd half-filled with ice helped soothe the ache in his hands. "I was hoping I'd get up there today and knock one out of the park."

"That could happen."

"Doubtful. I barely knocked a ball out of the infield today. I thought that if I got on base or drove home a few runs, I'd make Shane proud. I know he said I didn't have to be good, but I don't want to be dead weight. He's always taken care of me. Doing well out there is a small way to pay him back."

"Taking care of people seems to be his thing." Gabriel drew Jack's left hand onto his thigh and began massaging it.

"For me, it's deeper than that." He set his water aside and focused on Gabe's skilled fingers easing the ache. "Shane became my protector back in high school. I told you I was a scrawny kid. I didn't hit my growth spurt until my junior year. Anyway, in my freshman year, he sat next to me in history, and we had a few classes together. He was obviously a tough guy, like someone no one would want to mess with, you know what I mean? When I met him, I was worried he would be another bully, but he was nice. One day, I was getting shoved around by some guys, and he came right over, pushed his way in, and said if they wanted to fight someone, then they would fight him. No one had ever stood up for me before."

"Did they fight him?"

"One did, and one ran away. But the one who stayed didn't stand a chance. Shane was bigger, and once they started, you could tell it wasn't his first fight. He ended up with a black eye, but the other guy got a broken nose. They both ended up getting suspended. He sort of became my shadow after that and pulled me into his circle of friends. And the asshole kids at school and in the neighborhood eventually learned to leave me alone. So I have him to thank for that. Plus, he's been there for me ever since. The brother I never had."

"I'm glad he was there for you. Shane's a good guy. All of the Brennans are." Gabe switched to massaging Jack's right hand. "I met Ryan a few years ago at the gym. I was new to the neighborhood, didn't know anyone, and before I knew it, Ryan and Austin had adopted me, and soon I was getting invited to every Brennan family event. I didn't attend any for a long time because, in my experience, holidays spent with family were volatile situations to be avoided at all costs. Shane, Xavier, and Leo are how I wish my older brothers had been. That whole family... I grew up with criticism, insults, and fighting. The Brennans are like a safe haven of support, compliments, and hugs."

Jack turned his hand until he could easily hold Gabe's. "You made your own family out here."

"I guess I did." Gabe's gaze shifted over Jack's shoulder. "And here they are now."

Shane, Ryan, and Austin headed their way. Jack grinned and waved. They were his family too. Gratitude welled to overflowing, and he rose to greet them, pulling Gabe along.

Shane's gaze dropped to their joined hands. His brows rose, but he only said hello and hugged Gabe, then Jack. "You're here early."

"Gabe was helping me fix my batting stance. I can actually hit the ball now. Well, only sometimes, and it doesn't go far."

"Yeah?" Laughing, he swung an arm over Jack's shoulders. "You think you'd consider joining the team full-time for the fall season?"

He pulled away to study his friend's face. "You're serious. It's only been one game so far. Maybe we should see how I do for the next three games before talking about anything more."

"Okay, deal. But I'd like you to think about it." Shane tossed him a mitt. "Help me warm-up?"

They tossed the ball back and forth and got into a pretty good rhythm. Ryan, Austin, and Gabe were nearby, throwing the ball and laughing in their own warm-up. Jack's gaze kept tracking over to Gabe, but Shane didn't comment. Not even when both Jack and Gabe missed their respective catches because they were watching each other.

After that, Ryan snagged both balls. "We might as well make this one group, so those two," he pointed at Jack and Gabe, "don't end up with whiplash."

Heat flooded into him, but Jack laughed, and the warmth deepened when Gabe touched his arm as he walked by. As the warm-up resumed, he focused on throwing and catching as well as he could, needing to look good in front of Gabe.

And maybe he could fool even himself into becoming a better player.

When his two at-bats resulted in strikeouts during the game, Jack had the dark thought that maybe he could only hit a ball Gabe pitched, or maybe Gabe had thrown him some easy ones earlier. Everyone said his swing looked better, but he wasn't satisfied.

His next chance to bat came in the seventh inning. He replayed Gabriel's advice as he walked to the plate. The team needed two runs to win, and he desperately wanted to give them at least one. The final inning. His last chance to make something happen.

He fouled off the first ball for a strike. Swung and missed for the second strike. Then took a breath and readied for the next pitch.

The ball arced toward him. He shifted his weight, waited, and then swung as hard as he could.

Ping!

The ball soared over the infield.

Mouth open, Jack stared at its path. It bounced at the end of the dirt between the first and second baseman and continued into the outfield.

He'd actually hit it.

Shane's voice came from his right. "Run!"

He took off for first base.

"Drop the bat!" Shane's holler carried over his team-mates' cheers.

He released his hold as he ran and safely arrived at first base. Ryan stood by the fence, acting as first base coach. "Nice job. Now, when I tell you to go, take off, and keep your eye on Gabe. He'll let you know whether to hold up at second or to keep running."

Jack's heart beat fast, fueled by adrenaline. He sought out Gabriel on the third base side and waited for Ryan's instruction.

Austin was at the plate. Jack's gaze flicked to second base, which looked a lot farther away than it had a moment earlier.

Austin swung and hit. The ball shot through the air and sailed deep into the outfield.

"Run!" Ryan's voice propelled Jack forward. He pumped his legs as fast as he could. As his foot connected with the base, Gabriel from his position as third base coach waved his arm in a large circle, motioning for Jack to keep running. He kept his gaze on Gabriel, and fresh energy poured into him.

"Keep going," Gabe's voice called as Jack's foot made contact with third base. "Get home! Go!"

Jack ran, imagining for a second that he was a character in one of his books, and the killer was hot on his heels. He crossed the plate and turned to see Austin right behind him.

Bottom of the seventh. One out to go. But his job was done. Two runs clinched the victory.

He high-fived Austin and met his teammates in the dugout, accepting high-fives and back slaps and one-armed hugs as he made his way to Gabriel.

Eyes twinkling, Gabe swept him into a hug that lifted him

off of his feet. When he set him down, Gabe's hand caressed the back of Jack's neck. "You did so good."

Awareness sparked through his body. Jack made himself step away. "You deserve most of the credit. Thanks for helping me."

A cheer rose up around them, drowning out his words. Jack turned and bumped into Shane. His oldest friend beamed at him. "Game's over. Jack, you and Austin are getting a free drink at the bar. Great job out there."

"I'm happy I could help."

"We needed a win today. If we win the next two games, we'll make the playoffs." He plucked a cookie from the few remaining in the box. "Now, let's go celebrate."

The group left together and walked to the sports bar a few blocks away. It had scarred tables and dark floors and baseball highlights playing on every TV. Jack sat with Shane at the end of one long table. The rock music blaring from the speakers drowned out the conversations from the rest of the group.

Shane poured them both a glass of beer from a shared pitcher. "What's going on between you and Gabe?"

Jack set his drink down. He'd figured Shane would ask eventually. "I don't know. There's this connection… I can't explain it. When we were eating dinner in my kitchen Friday night—"

Shane's brows shot up. "You took him to your place? You never let people in your space right away. You dated Ken for two months before letting him hang out at your house."

That was true. "I don't know what to say. It's only been about a week, but it's been an intense week."

"You looked pretty into each other."

"Yeah." His gaze landed on Gabriel at the opposite end of the table, eyes crinkled as he laughed at something Ryan said.

"I don't want to see either of you get hurt."

He dragged his attention back to Shane. "I don't want that either."

Shane's gaze flicked between Jack and Gabriel a few more times. He opened his mouth, then closed it, then pressed his lips together as he focused on his beer. When his eyes lifted, clouded with concern, he sighed. "Look…"

Jack's stomach tightened. "What is it you want to say, Shane?"

"I'm friends with both of you. I know this is new, and it's intense, but just…" Shaking his head, he grimaced. "Damn, this is hard. It's not like either of you are dating someone who I have to warn off, but I'm still feeling really protective of both of you."

"You're a good friend."

A shrug and a grunt served as Shane's response. He shifted in his seat. "I want you to be happy. Gabe, too. Just… Have fun, but be careful. Okay?"

With a nod that hopefully reassured his friend. Jack picked up his drink. Hurting anyone was the last thing he wanted to do.

Gabe met his gaze and stood. He left a partially finished beer on the table and exchanged words and waves with everyone as he made his way closer. Obviously, he was leaving. Jack pushed his beer away as disappointment settled into a weight in his stomach.

When Gabe reached him, he leaned down, addressing both Jack and Shane. "I have to go. Ashley just messaged me. She needs me to do a delivery." His hand curled over Jack's shoulder. "Want to come, Jack? You haven't been on a delivery yet. It might be good for your novel."

The weight dissipated as warmth filled his chest. "I wouldn't miss it."

"I'm stopping home to shower first. I'll meet you at the bakery in an hour."

"I'll be there." Maybe they could grab dinner afterward, and see where the night took them. As Gabe left the bar, Jack pushed his chair back, ready to make his own exit. Shane's words echoed in his head.

Have fun, but be careful.

The characters in his novels barely heeded the warning to be careful. He was sure he could manage it in real life, so neither he nor Gabe would get hurt.

CHAPTER SEVEN

Raindrops dotted the windshield as Gabriel turned the delivery van into the community center's parking lot. He glanced at Jack. "We need to get the cake inside as fast as possible."

"I know. Water and sugar aren't a good combination. I'll hustle."

He parked as close as he could to the entrance. "Let's go."

The three-tier dinosaur-themed cake for six-year-old Connor was one of Gabe's favorites. Sebastian had done an amazing job sculpting the dinosaurs roaming the cake.

Gabe met Jack's gaze. "Keep it level, just like we did when leaving the bakery."

"I won't tip it or drop it. I swear."

They moved inside without issue and set the cake on a table laden with presents. The smile on Connor's face was the best reward. He excitedly pointed out and identified dinosaur after dinosaur. Another boy, a little bigger than Connor, ran to the table. With a smirk, he dragged his finger through the *Happy 6th Birthday Connor* message, smearing the letters.

"Hey!" Connor's lip trembled, and his eyes filled with tears.

The older boy ran away laughing as his mother screeched, "James, no video games for you for the rest of the week."

Connor's father crouched by his side, voice and expression firm. "Stop crying. Crying is for babies. Big boys don't cry."

Anger rose, hot and fierce, roaring through Gabriel like a dragon's fire. *Damn it.* Connor's father could have been his own. How many times had he heard the same toxic bullshit message over the years? He couldn't tell the six-year-old that his father was an unenlightened idiot, but he could repair a cake.

He rooted through his bag of emergency supplies then approached Connor with a smile. "Hey there, Connor, we can fix it."

Red-faced, the boy sniffed and wiped away the streaks of tears. "Really?"

"Yeah." He carefully filled in the swiped icing, adding thickness to the script to even out the letters. "What's your favorite dinosaur?"

The boy's lip wobbled again. "T-rex."

"What to help me make one?"

"Really?" Eyes wide, voice hopeful, he edged closer. "Can I?"

"Of course. You'll do great." He handed the kid the bag and then guided his hands as they piped a small green T-rex. Gabe switched to another, smaller bag and added some features and then a bright yellow C to the dinosaur's chest. "There. All fixed."

Connor beamed at him. "Thank you."

"Happy Birthday, buddy." He quickly packed up his supplies. Tension tightened his muscles, but he kept a professional smile in place and lightened his tone when he spoke his final words to Connor's mother, aware of Jack's gaze on him the entire time.

They didn't speak during the drive back to the bakery. Gabe was grateful for the silence. His mind was too full of memories, and his emotions were also on edge.

Jack unbuckled his seatbelt and shifted to facing Gabe when they parked the van. "You were great with that kid."

Gabe turned off the ignition. "He reminded me of myself at that age. What his older brother did is something mine would have done. And how his parents reacted is pretty much the same too. Most holidays and birthday parties turned into screaming matches at my house. I hated it. That's one of the reasons I don't go back to visit."

"I'm sorry." Jack's arms came around him, solid and strong and secure.

"Thanks." With a sigh, Gabe relaxed into the embrace. It had been years since he'd spent any time with his family, but the old hurts never truly went away.

After a long while, Jack pulled back and brushed his hand through Gabe's hair. "Want to come home with me? I forgot to get groceries, but we can order something."

The offer was sweet. But being surrounded by the horror memorabilia wasn't something Gabe wanted to deal with, not right now. "You haven't been to my place yet. Let's go there. I have chicken that needs to be cooked today anyway."

"Sounds good. More character inspiration too."

The walk home didn't take long. Gabe unlocked the front door and gestured for Jack to enter first.

Jack wandered straight to the bookcase in the living room.

"I'd been here a few times when Ryan lived here. I like how you've decorated."

"It's pretty simple." The big bookcase, comfortable chairs, and couch for reading or relaxing weren't fancy, but every single thing in his place made him smile. "I'll start dinner."

"I'll help." Jack followed him into the kitchen. He chopped vegetables and cleaned up while Gabe cooked the chicken and pasta, and kept the conversation easy and light throughout the preparation and eating of the meal, focusing on books they'd both read. After they'd finished eating, he insisted on washing the dishes.

When the last dish had been put away, they moved into the living room with bottles of beer. Gabriel handed Jack the remote. "Find something."

Jack flipped through the channel menu and stopped at a horror movie. "This one is so good. It's my all-time favorite. What do you think?"

"Uh, sure. We can watch it." Mentally cringing, Gabe forced a smile. Jack was the guest, and the guest got to choose. He hadn't seen that movie before, maybe it wouldn't be too scary or gruesome. "I'll make some popcorn."

Before long, they were settled on the couch with the lights turned off, and the bowl of popcorn between them.

The movie's music was simple in arrangement but effectively eerie. Every time it raised in intensity, Gabriel took that as his cue to look at something other than the screen.

As the killer flashed on the screen and his victim ran in terror, he directed his attention to the popcorn. Lights flickered from the TV and illuminated his hand so close to Jack's. He stroked the back of Jack's fingers. Long fingers, perfect for playing the piano. Did Jack play? There was still so much Gabe didn't know.

With a smile, Jack set the bowl on the coffee table and then moved closer to Gabe and wrapped his arm around Gabe's shoulders. For the next few minutes, as the characters on screen wandered around an old graveyard at night, he leaned into Jack's warmth and soaked up the sweetness of having Jack so close.

An ominous change in the movie's score meant it was time to look away once again. Gabriel traced a pattern over Jack's thigh. Figure eights and swirls as shrieks came from the speakers, then as the sounds of clanging metal and more cries came, he skated his fingers higher. Touching Jack was his favorite new distraction.

The arm around his shoulders moved. Jack's fingers slid into his hair and gently tugged until Gabe's attention shifted from Jack's thigh to his face. In the dim light, Jack gazed at him under lids heavy with arousal. Lips parted, he directed Gabe closer until their mouths were inches apart, and they were sharing breath.

The space between them was like a magnetic field, and Gabe was powerless to resist the pull. His heart beat faster as he edged closer.

Jack's lips brushed over his mouth, once, twice, then again as he brought his other hand to cup Gabe's jaw. Long fingers stroked like Gabe was something treasured that needed special care.

Their tongues met in languid kisses, hot and wet, and deep.

And then, with a groan, Jack devoured him. His tongue plunged inside, sweeping and stroking and demanding. The force of Jack's kiss took his breath away. Gabe tangled his fingers in the soft curls and returned the kiss, pushing to get closer. What had started as a distraction became his sole purpose. He needed Jack.

Jack's lips on him. Jack's hands on him. Just Jack, everywhere.

For so long, he'd dreamed about what kissing Jack and holding him would be like. Jack, real and *here*, and in his arms, far surpassed any fantasy.

Fighting through the passion clouding his vision, Gabe continued his exploration, his hands traveling over Jack's chest and stomach. Heat seeped through the thin material of his shirt. He pushed the fabric up and out of the way, sliding underneath and caressing his fingers over even hotter skin.

When Jack's thighs spread wider in invitation, Gabe took his time, moving to trace his inner thighs before finally skating his fingers over the prominent bulge in the rough denim. Slowly squeezing Jack's cock, he nipped at Jack's lips and captured each gasp.

Jack drew Gabe's lower lip in and scraped it with his teeth. Shivering as his blood sang with desire, Gabe tugged Jack's shirt up and off, tossing it to the floor, revealing smooth skin and Jack's lanky frame. A sprinkling of blond hair covered Jack's chest. "I love the way you look. I've pictured this so many times."

Moaning, Jack hit a button on the remote and then dropped it to the floor. The sounds coming from the speakers stopped, but light still emanated from the screen.

Gabe pushed to kneeling. He straddled Jack, directing their lips together once more, and took full control of the kiss.

Cool air hit his skin as Jack pushed his shirt up. Gabe pulled back just enough to help Jack rid him of the material. As the writer's gaze tracked over his body, Gabe puffed out his chest, hoping Jack liked what he saw.

Jack's eyes gleamed as he traced sure hands over Gabe's chest and stomach. Closing his eyes, Gabe absorbed the feeling of Jack's hands on his body. Arousing, exciting, there were too many feelings mixing together, but it was intoxicating. The heated pads tracked lower, and Gabe's cock jerked as they grew closer to his waistband.

They skimmed lower in the tiniest increments, as though Jack was waiting for permission. He watched Gabe's face, giving him plenty of time to decide what he wanted to happen next.

Gabe nodded and kissed him and shifted his hips so that Jack's fingers brushed where Gabe wanted to feel them most.

Holding his gaze, Jack stroked over his swollen member, the touch muted by the layers of his jeans and boxers. Slow and steady as Gabe rocked into the touch. "Lay down with me?"

Gabe pulled back, hard and aching. He waited as Jack positioned himself along the cushions and then stretched out beside him. Their bare torsos met, and he shivered at the sensation of being skin on skin with Jack. He traced a finger along Jack's cheek and skated it over that pillow soft mouth. They were close enough to feel every inch of each other, and part of him still couldn't believe it.

Jack... long and lean and stretched out beside him. He captured Jack's mouth, drawing out kiss after kiss, while his hands explored skin like velvet and firm muscles.

On a moan, Jack attacked his mouth, thrusting his tongue past Gabe's lips, mimicking the action of his hips. Gabe met him every step, grinding their cocks together.

Needing more friction and less clothing, he reached down, but Jack's hands beat him to it. "Let me."

Jack popped the button and glided the zipper down, and ran a fingertip over Gabe's cock as it pushed through the opening in his jeans. Jack's eyes were slits as he opened his own jeans. Gabe watched the slow reveal. The dim light from the TV picked up the light contrast of Jack's underwear.

Grasping Jack's hips, raking his hands along the writer's ribcage, then sliding down to grip his ass, Gabe couldn't get close enough. Needing more room, he maneuvered until Jack lay underneath him.

Kiss after kiss after kiss, they rocked against each other. Jack's hands roamed Gabe's chest, tweaking his nipples, making him groan and then tracing a path down the center of Gabe's body. He pushed the jeans and boxers down a few inches and worked Gabe's length with both hands. Biting his lip, Gabe arched into Jack's touch. His fantasies truly hadn't come close.

Desperate to return the pleasure, Gabe freed Jack from the confines of his clothing, pushing the jeans and shorts down Jack's hips. Leaning on one elbow, he stroked Jack slowly, watching as brown eyes widened and then closed in a gasp of Gabe's name. Both of Jack's hands dove into Gabe's hair and dragged him into a kiss.

His skin was too hot. His body was demanding release, and he wanted to bring Jack over the edge with him. He closed his hand over their cocks as they rocked harder, breathless between kisses. Gabe tightened his grip. "Let go for me, Jack."

Jack's hands dug into Gabe's back. He arched his hips, groaning as his release coated Gabe's hand. The extra lubrication and the dazed beauty of Jack's face sent Gabe over the edge. Pleasure quaked through his body as Jack's mouth closed over his and swallowed the sounds of his release.

When thinking became easier again, and his limbs felt less like rubber, Gabe grabbed his shirt from the floor and used it to clean them up.

Jack stretched, rubbing their bodies together again. "I'm too boneless to move."

"You can stay over." He liked the idea of going to sleep in Jack's arms. "Do you want to go upstairs?"

"In a little while." Jack snagged the remote and with one click, plunged the room into darkness. His lips and fingers returned to trace over Gabe's skin. "For now, staying right here feels perfect."

Gabe had to agree. Wrapped up in Jack, there wasn't any place else he'd rather be.

A crash jolted Gabriel wide awake. Heart pounding, he sat up. Jack wasn't beside him in the bed. He peered around the darkened room. Jack's clothes weren't on the dresser.

The sound of something being dragged across the floor downstairs sent a chill down his spine. Was it Jack, or had Jack gone home? There had been a rash of break-ins in the neighborhood the previous summer. He cursed himself now for not getting an alarm system.

He'd left his phone on the kitchen table. No way could he call for help without it.

Ears pricked for more sounds, he climbed out of bed and pulled on a pair of workout shorts over his boxers, scanning the room for a weapon. The Louisville Slugger in his closet, signed by three members of the Phillies World Series team, was his best option.

He inched his way through the darkness and eased the closet open. The bat would do some damage.

More sounds came from downstairs, water running in the sink, and then the fridge opening.

It had to be Jack. Right?

His thoughts flashed to the slasher movie. Maybe he was

stupid for investigating a bump in the night. But, damn it, this was his home. He couldn't just cower in bed.

At the top of the stairs, he paused again. The kitchen light was on. Someone was definitely in there.

"Jack?" He called out despite the pulse pounding in his throat.

Silence echoed back.

Fear washed icy over his skin. He descended the stairs, careful to keep his footsteps light.

A thud came from the kitchen.

Holding tight to his bat and his courage, Gabriel ran into the kitchen, bat poised to strike.

Jack jumped up from the table, upending his chair. Eyes wild, he yanked earbuds from his ears. "What the hell?"

Chest heaving, heartbeat hammering, Gabe lowered the bat. "Why didn't you answer me when I called? I thought you were a burglar."

"Shit. I'm sorry." Hand pressed over his chest, he squeezed his eyes shut for a moment, and then bent and righted the chair. "I couldn't sleep and came down here to write. I didn't mean to wake you."

"The crash did. What was it?"

"I broke a glass when I got a drink of water. I'll replace it."

"Don't worry about that." Gabe set the bat against the wall. His heart rate slowly returned to normal. "I'm glad it's you and not some psychopath wearing a mask."

Jack's brows drew together and then understanding lightened across his face. "The movie we watched tonight."

"We didn't watch that much of it…" Gabe crossed his arms over his chest. Despite his embarrassment, he had to be honest. "I have an overactive imagination. So I don't watch or read things like that. Whenever I do, for hours afterward, I keep thinking about how anything could be lurking here in the shadows or behind furniture or doors. Stupid, I know, but—"

"Not stupid," Jack corrected, his voice firm and sympathy softening his gaze. "It's not, and I'd never suggest otherwise. But someone obviously has."

Gabe's chest throbbed and he blinked away the burning sensation building behind his eyes. He nodded, but didn't elaborate. He didn't want to get into more stories about his family.

Jack's chest rose as he inhaled a deep breath. His shoulders were tight and his hands clasped into fists like he was imagining rushing into battle to defend Gabe from the people he didn't wish to name. He released the breath slowly, rolled his shoulders, and opened his hands, and the tension drained away. A smile formed as he studied Gabe's face, transforming the last of the storm in his eyes to gentler seas. "I'll tell you something. There have been a few times where I've written something that's freaked even me out. I might admit to sleeping with the lights on a time or two."

He gaped at the man. "Really?"

"Sure. Some of my favorite horror authors say the same thing. Our imaginations form too many shapes in the dark and our days are spent writing about nightmare situations." Jack closed his notebook and rounded the table. He slipped his arms around Gabe's torso, affection lighting up his features. "You were brave coming in here to face an unknown."

Heat charge up Gabe's neck and flushed into his cheeks and ears. "There's a fine line between being brave and being stupid. What if you hadn't been you? The first rule of staying alive in one of those movies is to not investigate strange noises."

"If you're still thinking about that movie, I'm happy to

take your mind off of it." He pulled Gabe tighter into his embrace, wrapping him in safety and security, and his lips settled against Gabe's, soft and sweet.

With a sigh, Gabe relaxed into Jack. His hands roamed over the T-shirt covered torso and pressed Jack's body tight to his own. He couldn't get close enough. The kiss deepened, their tongues stroked together, and his nerve endings tingled as want and need flared to life.

Jack lifted his head, eyes shining, and skimmed his fingers along Gabe's cheek. "Let's go to bed. By the time I finish, you won't be thinking of anything except you and me. I promise."

CHAPTER EIGHT

Hand in hand, Jack walked to the bedroom with Gabriel. He felt awful for giving the man such a scare, and even worse because he figured he knew who hadn't been so kind to Gabe in the past about his imagination and why he didn't like to read or watch scary things.

The bedside lamp cast a soft glow on rumpled sheets. The air-conditioning kicked on with a faint hum. Gabe put the baseball bat in the closet and then turned to Jack with his hand outstretched.

Palm met palm, and Jack drew Gabe into his arms. He trailed his lips over Gabe's neck, raising goosebumps. Gabe shivered and pulled him closer and nudged his nose against Jack's cheek until their lips met. Jack poured all of the passion, all of the promise he'd made to take care of Gabriel, into that kiss. When he drew back, he nodded toward the bed. "Lay down on your stomach."

Brow raised, Gabe stretched out in the center of the mattress and tucked a pillow under his head. Jack took a moment to admire the play of light over the dips and planes of toned muscles, then he straddled Gabe's waist and placed his hands on Gabe's bare back.

Massaging his way across the shoulders and neck and upper back, he took his time, reveling in Gabe's every contented sigh as tension released. He scooted back a few inches and continued the massage across the mid and low back, alternately digging in with his thumbs and pressing in with his palms. "This is what I wanted to do that day at the bakery when you were rushing to complete the re-do of the wedding cake. The little massage I managed to get in wasn't enough."

"It helped me." Gabe turned his head and adjusted his pillow. "This feels amazing. It's probably good that you didn't do all of this then. I would've either melted into a puddle or dragged you off someplace to take things to the next level. Either way, we would've missed the deadline."

"The next level, hmm?" He grinned, amused and aroused. "Is that code for sex?"

Reaching underneath himself, Gabe grunted. "You know it is. I'm already more than halfway hard. Like you said that day, your hands are good for more than just writing."

That reminder had so many ideas sparking to life… all of them starring Gabriel. "Have you ever had sex at a bakery?"

"No. But I can't say that I haven't thought about it."

"Would you?"

Twisting, he raised himself onto one elbow and met Jack's gaze. His eyes glittered like a sparkling sea, invited him to dive in and stay. "If I had the right muse."

"If that's an invitation… I'm there." Jack shifted forward, placing his hands on the mattress at either side of Gabriel's shoulders and pressed a kiss to Gabriel's waiting lips. "Speaking of muses… He walks in beauty like the night, of cloudless climes and starry skies; and all that's best of dark and bright, meet in his aspect and his eyes; thus mellowed to that tender light which heaven to gaudy day denies."

Gabe's eyes widened and his lips parted as surprise stole over his features. He threaded a hand through Jack's hair. "Taking liberties with Byron's words?"

"Hey, as far as I'm concerned, Byron would be all for adapting to suit the proper muse."

"I'm so turned on right now."

He wasn't the only one. Desire consumed every cell in Jack's body, even his heart seemed to beat Gabe's name. "One shade the more, one ray the less, had half impaired the nameless grace, which waves in every raven tress, or softly lightens o'er his face."

On a soft moan, Gabe shifted until he was on his back. "We're living out one of my fantasies."

"Are we?" A memory surfaced of Gabe and him in Jack's bedroom, and their conversation over Jack's volume of poetry, and his suggestion to Gabe: *Maybe you'll read some and think of me.* And Gabe's response: *Who says I haven't already?* "Want me to keep going?"

"I can think of other, more intimate things to do with our mouths. Kiss me."

Jack obliged, dropping down to meet Gabriel's waiting lips. The kiss went on for ages, a leisurely exploration as passion built.

He lifted his head and moved back until he straddled Gabe's waist, and his arms were free to roam and play and excite. Watching Gabe's face, he traced patterns over the sexy man's arms and torso, studying and memorizing what caused every sigh and shiver. Then he followed across the same expanse of skin with kisses that nipped and soothed. Shifting farther back, he settled in between Gabe's legs and rested his hands on thigh muscles that jumped and flexed. "I want to taste you."

Gabe licked his lips and nodded. Smile wicked, Jack knelt and eased the shorts and boxers down Gabe's legs.

Gabe lay before him, all strength and defined muscles, from his broad shoulders to his powerful thighs. He tossed the clothes to the floor and then skated his fingers up Gabriel's thighs, over his hips and up to his chest, before reversing course down that taunt stomach. Finally, he wrapped his hand around Gabe's cock.

Moaning, Gabe lifted his hips as the slow strokes started from base to tip. Jack lowered his head and teased a path of kisses down the dark trail from Gabe's navel to the base of his dick, caught up in Gabe's sharp inhale and the way his stomach sucked in as Jack's lips headed south.

Gabe's cock bumped his chin, begging for attention. Jack lapped at the fluid leaking from the head and glanced up. Gabriel watched him, eyes blazing as electricity sparked between them. His hand slid down his torso and brushed across Jack's cheek. "I've pictured this so many times."

"I have too. I'll do my best to make sure reality is better than fantasy." Jack swallowed him down, inch by inch. Relaxing his throat, he took him all the way in.

Gabe cried out, bucking his hips as he held on to Jack's hair. Jack worked the length with mouth and hands, then pulled back and took in just the head, teasing Gabe's slit with his tongue. His fingers roamed, pumping and stroking the shaft, teasing his balls, then farther back to discover new spots of pleasure. Gabe widened his legs, opening himself for more of Jack's touch.

The sounds leaving Gabe's lips, the moans and gasps, the shaky breaths and whispers of Jack's name, the clawing hands and lifting hips and clenching muscles, all drove him on. He used every trick, every secret, every bit of knowledge to saturate Gabriel in sensation. Then he did it again. And again. And again. And again. And again.

"Jack." Gabe clutched at his back and his hair, grunting as his body jerked through his orgasm.

Jack kept kissing and touching, drawing it out, swallowing everything Gabe gave him.

Soon, the hands in his hair gentled to caresses. "Jack?"

Lips swollen, Jack eased back. "Yeah?"

"Lay down." Voice hoarse, he nudged Jack's shoulder. "Let me make you feel good too."

The blood in his head drained south. He was already hard and aching and craving Gabe's touch. Jack quickly shed his clothes and then joined Gabe on the mattress. Want overwhelmed him. "Kiss me?"

"Of course." Gabe rolled on top of him and dove into kissing Jack. The full length, warm weight of Gabe without any barrier of clothing was a delicious sensation.

Gabe shifted downward, trailing kisses along Jack's chin, his neck, and his chest. Jack raised onto his elbows and watched. Gabriel was kissing him, touching him, and getting increasingly intimate. His muscles quivered under Gabe's attention. The sexy baker wasn't the only one who'd fantasized about this moment.

The feel of Gabe's beard against the sensitive skin of his thighs almost made him lose control. So did the sight of Gabe's hand wrapped around his cock. And when Gabe's lips and tongue teased along the sensitive skin, and he captured Jack's gaze, Jack had to pinch himself to make sure he wasn't dreaming. Leaning back, he reveled in Gabriel's command of his body. One hand massaged Jack's balls, the other kept stroking his shaft, and Gabe's lips and tongue were *everywhere,* sucking and licking and hot and wet and driving him higher and higher.

Jack arched back, lost in the sensations destroying him. His broken moan pierced the silence as he thrashed on the pillows.

The temptation to let go and give himself over to the heated talents of Gabe's mouth was strong, but Jack still had more pleasure to give. He gentled his hold on Gabe's hair and shoulder and slowly guided him back. "Come up here."

"With pleasure." Gabe kissed his way up Jack's body, and when their mouths came together, Jack groaned at the taste himself on Gabe's tongue. He pulled Gabriel against him and trailed his fingers over every inch of skin he could reach.

Gabriel trembled under his hands. He leaned across the bed and fumbled in the bedside table and came back with a bottle of lube and a condom. Kissing Jack deeply, he pressed both items into his hand. "Please."

The weight of responsibility, of trust, was huge. Jack took another kiss. With shaking fingers, he opened the lube while Gabe rolled onto his stomach.

Settled between Gabe's thighs once again, Jack drizzled the cold liquid onto his palm. He rubbed his hands together to warm it and then coated Gabe's entrance. Placing a kiss between Gabe's shoulder blades, he gently worked his way inside. So hot, so tight. His cock jerked, wanting in. He added more fingers as he stroked Gabe's prostate and more kisses down his spine to match every gasp and moan leaving Gabriel's lips.

Gabe pushed back, grinding his hips against Jack's erection. "I'm ready. I want to feel you."

"I want that too. To feel you all around me." He ripped open the condom and rolled it on and added more lube, and then guided his throbbing cock to Gabe's entrance. He paused there, taking in the way the lamplight cast a glow on Gabe's skin and how warm Gabe felt against him. This wasn't a random night with a random stranger, this was Gabriel. Strong and sensitive and sexy and sweet Gabriel.

"Jack…" Gabe rolled his hips. "Please…"

Heartbeat pounding, he pushed inside. Slower than his body was demanding, slower than maybe Gabe wanted. They both groaned. Jack grabbed hold of Gabe's hips, fingers digging into the skin as he inched farther and farther until he was fully seated.

Tight, hot, and so very perfect.

He wasn't going to last long. Biting his lip, he fought for control and stroked his hands over Gabriel's back. "Let me know when you're ready for me to move."

On a moan, Gabe squeezed around him. "I've been ready, Jack. Please."

Desire buzzed steadily in his blood, pulsing with every beat of his heart. He pulled out almost all the way and pushed back in. Not fast enough for Gabe, as the man bucked his hips and fisted his hands in the sheets and growled for *more*. Gripping Gabe's shoulder and hip, Jack slid out and in again, holding tight as he increased his pace.

They rocked together, harder and faster, to the soundtrack of a squeaking mattress. Skin grew slick with sweat, and Jack's hands slid along Gabe's sides, seeking purchase. He fell forward, taking Gabe down with him. Gabe grabbed his hand and kissed it. Linking their hands together, Jack pushed back inside Gabe's heat, anchored by the fingers curled tight around his own.

As Jack drew closer to losing control, the need to make Gabe release first became his sole purpose. He reached for Gabe's cock, met Gabe's hand, and together, they stroked until Gabe came with a broken moan of Jack's name.

That sound alone was the hottest, sweetest, most amazing thing he'd ever heard. Gabe's muscles clamped around him.

Desperately seeking his release, Jack thrust his hips into that impossibly tight heat. Pleasure rushed over his skin, blazed like a firestorm through his blood, and finally consumed him.

Panting, he collapsed onto Gabe. When his heartbeat leveled, he managed to roll to the side. He dealt with the condom, wrapping it in a tissue and tossed it in the small trash can by the bed.

Soft kisses covered his neck, and Gabe's strong arm wrapped around him and pulled Jack into his chest. He turned his head and sought Gabe's lips in a languid kiss.

Long moments later, Gabe turned out the light. Jack drifted to sleep, surrounded by cool darkness and Gabriel's warmth.

The alarm clock's blare yanked him from dreams. Jack blinked his eyes open as Gabriel reached across him to silence the wail. Was it five o'clock already? He felt like he'd just fallen asleep. Of course, they pretty much had. He'd pulled out all the stops to bring Gabe every bit of pleasure to make up for scaring him so much at three AM.

Gabe's sleep-warmed body shifted across Jack's in the most delicious way. Jack wrapped his arms around him, nuzzling the side of his neck. "Morning."

"Morning." With a smile and a sigh, Gabe cupped Jack's cheek. "Sleep okay?"

He nodded and ran his hands over the sculpted planes of Gabriel's back. "You?"

"With you next to me? After what we did last night? Oh, yeah." Eyes heavy-lidded, Gabe lowered his head and trailed his lips over Jack's collar bone and neck. "I wish we could stay here all morning. I'm sorry to have to kick you out so early, but I need to open the shop."

"No problem. I need to get home and get to writing." But even as he spoke, he arched into Gabriel's body. Parts of him were very interested in picking up right where they'd left off last night, and having an encore performance. He spread his legs wider, groaning when Gabe's thighs settled between his and nudged them even farther apart. Gabriel was bigger and broader, and Jack wanted to be the center of attention of all of that raw power. Between lazy kisses and the slow rolling of hips, he lost himself in Gabriel.

Beep. Beep. Beep.

The blare sounded again, an angry intrusion reminding him of obligations and responsibilities.

Moaning, Gabe dropped his head into the crook of Jack's neck and shoulder. "I really have to get up now."

Palming the soft skin at Gabe's neck, Jack massaged the area while his other hand traced lazy circles over Gabe's back. "I'd suggest showering together, but that would just slow us down even more."

"If I were in there with you, trust me, we wouldn't be getting out for a long time." Gabriel raised his head. "Not that I'm opposed to trying that out when I have more than ten minutes to spare."

"I'll hold you to it." Jack brushed his lips against Gabe's one more time. "Go shower. I'll make you some coffee."

Gabe rolled off him with a smile, and Jack watched him until Gabe disappeared into the hall, followed by the sound of the bathroom door closing behind him.

He tugged the covers over the bed, dressed, and then padded downstairs. Starting the coffee didn't seem like enough, not after the night they'd shared. Rolling with the odd domestic urge to feed Gabe, he searched the fridge and found a bag of whole-grain cinnamon raisin bagels and a package of cream cheese.

Perfect.

He popped two into the toaster oven. Peeking into cabinets yielded a tube of wax paper and a collection of food storage containers, stacked in size order. Jack slathered the cream cheese on the bagels, wrapped them up, then poured coffee into a travel mug for Gabe, and set everything on the counter.

Now that he was awake, the story slid into his thoughts, and his fingers itched to get back to work. His notebook on the table called him like a beacon. He sat and dashed down notes for a scene, only stopping when Gabe came into the room a while later.

Hair still damp from his shower, Gabe kissed Jack's cheek. He wore that pair of jeans that hugged him perfectly and a white Bliss Bakery T-shirt with yellow lettering. He glanced at the counter and did a double-take. "You made breakfast for me?"

"It's just a bagel, but yeah. You always seem worried about whether I've eaten, so I'm returning the favor."

"You made one for yourself, too, right?"

Caught between laughter and exasperation, he held up his wrapped bagel. "Right here."

"Okay." Smiling, Gabe kissed him again. "Thank you."

Jack packed up his things and walked with Gabriel to the front door. He slid his hands up Gabe's strong chest and framed his face. "Last night was great. I'll talk to you soon."

Gabe nodded and hauled him with his free hand. "Good luck with your writing."

The kiss goodbye was hard and fast and left Jack wanting more, but he stepped back and then followed Gabe outside and made himself turn in the direction of home.

Walking wasn't fast enough. He ended up jogging. The words were flowing, and he didn't want to lose them. Once inside the house, he shut off his phone, started the coffee, set up his laptop at the kitchen table, and then let the words consume him.

CHAPTER NINE

The clang of exercise machines, the thud of free weights hitting the floor, and the hum of treadmills were Gabriel's soundtrack. Working out his body had always worked to quiet his mind, but not even a ninety-minute sweat session following the full day of being run ragged at the bakery was enough. Dripping with sweat and muscles burning, he finished with his kettlebell and placed it on the rack.

Time to hit the showers, then dive into a book and close out the outside world. Maybe that wasn't the most exciting way to mark turning another year older, but emotional, mental, and physical exhaustion had won out.

He wiped a fresh towel over his face and neck as he turned away from the rows of weights. The Brennan family's gym was filled with the usual late afternoon crowd. He nodded to a few of the regulars, thrilled for Ryan and Shane that the gym had grown to become one of the most popular facilities in South Philly.

Austin and Ryan crossed the vast expanse of the floor, heading right toward him. Austin had been busy working with one of his personal training clients when Gabe had arrived, and Ryan had been on front desk duty. Gabe lifted his hand in a wave.

They'd both asked him a few times over the past week what he wanted to do for his birthday, and both were supportive when he'd said that he'd hoped to spend it with Jack, and was waiting on word.

Ryan caught him in a half-hug. "Happy Birthday! What are your plans for tonight? Are you seeing Jack?"

He shook his head. He'd sent two messages. One on Monday morning, wishing Jack good luck with writing, and another on Tuesday, letting Jack know about his birthday and asking if Jack wanted to celebrate it with him. He'd thought the message had been cute, non-threatening, and flirty. Jack hadn't responded to either. Gabe wasn't sure what that meant. He didn't want to let himself worry whether he'd messed up things with Jack, yet, that thought kept popping up every free minute.

Ryan exchanged a split-second glance with Austin, and then he smiled bright and wide. "Cool, that means you're free to have dinner with us."

The last thing he wanted was for them to catch him moping. "I think I'll just stay in. Have an early night. Maybe get started on the new novel I bought."

"No." Crossing muscular arms over an equally muscular chest emblazoned with the gym's logo, Austin shook his head. "You can't spend your birthday alone."

"Exactly," Ryan chimed in. "Spend it with us."

"I…" His phone rang, interrupting his search for an excuse as to why he'd want to spend a birthday alone when he hadn't in previous years. "It's my parents."

The brightness in Ryan's smile dimmed as his face creased into lines of concern. He nudged Austin, and they both took a step back. "We'll get out of your way."

Gabe grabbed the phone and walked toward the wall of windows facing the busy street. He quickly did the math in his head. The last time they'd talked had easily been a month or two earlier. "Hello?"

"Gabriel, we're calling to wish you a happy birthday." His mother's voice was cheerful, and didn't hold its usual tiredness.

"Thanks, Mom." In the background, he heard his father's voice and his eldest brother's. His father wasn't usually home at this time of day.

"Hold on, I'll give this to your father. I'm in the middle of getting ready to head in for my shift."

Gabe strained to listen as the phone was passed, but nothing beyond a heavy sigh came through the brief, muffled conversation.

"Gabe?" Age or more likely temperament had given his father's terse voice a new gruffness. "Happy Birthday."

"Thanks." He gripped the phone and searched for something to fill the awkward silence. "How's work?"

"Grueling. I earned this vacation day, that's for sure. You still making cakes for a living?"

"Yeah, Dad." He sighed and steeled himself. Every conversation that brought up the bakery also brought up his father's continued ire that Gabe was *"throwing that education I broke my back for into the trash."* They hadn't been happy with his decision to not go into teaching, but while his mother seemed like she'd moved on from her disappointment, his father always harped that Gabe had wasted his money and Gabe's own time pursuing a degree that had gone unused.

"You know, your cousin just became a tenured professor. He did his old man proud."

"That's nice for Clayton."

"That could've been you."

Gabe didn't want to deal with defending his decision again today. Maybe he could cut off what sounded like the start of a tirade. "We don't know that for sure. Look, Dad, I know you said no to my offer to pay you and Mom back for the tuition before, but if you've changed your mind, I'm still willing to do that. I can send you a bit every month."

A huff flooded out of the speaker. "I'll repeat what I told you the last time you offered. Save your money. Don't be stupid."

It was a no-win situation.

His eldest brother's voice boomed in the background, "Dad, let's *go*. We need to hit the road if we want to get there for batting practice."

Gabe jumped on the change of subject. Baseball was only one they could talk about for any length of time without issue. "You and Jim are going to the Reds game?"

"No. The Dragons game. And traffic's going to be a bitch. Here's your mother again."

"Thanks," Gabe said into the muffled noises of the phone being handed off once again.

"Gabriel? Sorry, but I really have to go. I need to be at work in an hour."

"Sure, Mom. Well… Thanks for calling me."

"Enjoy your day."

The line went dead. Gabe lowered the phone and stared out the window, feeling stupid for getting his hopes up, annoyed at himself for caring, and frustrated that sixty seconds of conversation put him right back into the lost, left out ache he'd felt so often over the years.

A family passed by, and both parents were talking to their kids and smiling. The two smallest boys were holding the woman's hands, and the older child pushed a stroller that held a waving toddler. The man carried yet another toddler and ruffled the older boy's hair as they both laughed together. Gabe leaned on the sill, watching until they moved out of sight. Why couldn't his own family have been that way?

"Gabe?" A gentle hand touched his shoulder.

He jolted and turned around.

Ryan stood before him, eyes full of compassion. "You okay?"

"Sure." Tucking his phone into his pocket, he yanked the towel from his shoulder with his other hand then rubbed it over his face once more. His friends knew how things with his family really were. They understood. But that didn't mean that Gabe wanted to talk about it.

"At least they called, right?"

"Right." But he couldn't shake the feeling that for them, today, he may have been an afterthought. "Listen, I'm heading out."

"Austin and I really want to do something nice for you tonight." Not above begging, Ryan could turn on puppy dog eyes to melt the hardest of hearts. He gestured toward Austin, who was back at the front desk, signing someone in. "Please? It'll be low-key. Dinner at my place in an hour. What do you say?"

Glancing between his two best friends, and thinking about how they had always been there for each other, the idea of solitude didn't hold the alluring power it had minutes earlier. Being alone with his thoughts was probably the last thing he needed. Thank goodness for his friends. They knew him better than he knew himself at times.

He bit back his suggestion that they just keep things easy, and stay at his place and order something. Ryan loved cooking and entertaining. It was one of the ways he showed love. "Okay, dinner sounds great. Let me shower and change, and I'll meet you at your place."

"Awesome." Beaming a smile, Ryan sent Austin a thumbs up, and then clapped Gabe on the back. "You'll have fun. I promise."

An hour after leaving his friends at the gym, Gabe rang the bell at the house Ryan shared with Everson. The pep talk he'd given himself on the short walk over had helped. He was damn lucky to have the friends that he did, and he wasn't going to let anything ruin their time together.

The door swung open, and Ryan waved him inside. "Right on time."

"Is Austin here yet?" Gabe answered his own question a second later as he stepped into the foyer. In the adjoining living room, under a huge *Happy Birthday* banner and a large bouquet of balloons, Austin sat with Everson and Ryan's dad, Mike, on the couch. Beside them, Xavier and Ashley and Leo and Kelsey flanked various chairs. Even Xavier's dog, Rocky, was there.

His mouth fell open, and he shuffled back a step and grabbed onto Ryan's arm. They were all there to celebrate *him*? "Low-key, hmm?"

Wearing a wide grin, eyes gleaming, Ryan hugged him. "Just family. So, yeah. Austin and I are finishing up in the kitchen, so just hang out here and relax."

Gabe held on, squeezing his thanks into the embrace. "I don't know what to say. You're… This… It's… Thank you."

"What are friends for?" Ryan released him and then ushered him into the living room. "Look who I found, everyone."

Everyone stood, waving hello, calling out greetings,

crowding closer for hugs, and Gabe had a *Happy Birthday* wished to him from every direction.

"Whoa, hey, thanks, everyone." He accepted a hug from Ashley first, his heart filling with the warmth emanating from the circle of people surrounding him. Kelsey hugged him next, then Leo, and then Rocky jumped up on him. Laughing, Gabe rubbed a hand over the Rottweiler's head. "Hey there, boy."

Xavier joined them and kept one hand on Rocky's collar. "Down, Rocky. Sorry, Gabe, he's excited. All of his favorite people are in the same place."

"I'm glad he's here." And so very glad to be included in the list of favorite people. "Glad you're all here. It's a great surprise."

Mike lumbered over, nearly as tall and broad as all of his boys. "Like we'd miss your birthday. It's written on my calendar, the same as all the rest of this group."

Gabe's throat thickened. "Thanks, Mike."

"Happy Birthday, kid." Mike's hug brought on the threat of tears, but Gabe willed them away. He'd never once heard an *I love you,* or had gotten so much as a hug from his own father, and Mike Brennan was the complete opposite: hugs and back claps were doled out freely to all of his sons, he was never stingy with expressions of love and praise, and Gabriel had been a recipient of that warmth from the very beginning.

Xavier motioned for Gabe to sit in the empty space between him and Leo. "Ashley was just telling us before you came in about how you all were run off your feet today at the shop. Sounds like it was a brutal day. You'll probably sleep good tonight."

On Xavier's other side, Ashley rubbed Rocky's head. The dog had nestled his way between them. "This one woke us up at one-thirty, howling at a cat. I hope he won't see or hear anything interesting tonight. I'm exhausted."

"I'm opening tomorrow, so maybe you can sleep in a bit." Gabe rested his head on the cushion. Hopefully, sleep would come quickly for him, and he wouldn't toss and turn all night thinking about Jack.

The doorbell rang, and Rocky bolted toward it. Xavier rose, huffing out a sigh, and followed the dog. "Calm down, boy." Then called over his shoulder, "It's like he knows who is behind the door."

Gabe's heart leaped into his throat as he counted the people in the room and realized who was missing.

Shane.

Would it be just Shane at the door, or possibly also Jack?

His heartbeat kicked into a higher gear, and Gabe sat up straight, trying to look unaffected.

Xavier came back, followed by a laughing Shane and an overexcited Rocky. The dog raced around the room twice in a crazy loop.

"Hey, bud, happy birthday." Maneuvering around the dog, Shane leaned over and ruffled Gabe's hair. "Sorry I'm late. I had to go over some things with our newest assistant manager."

He smiled and nodded and asked none of the questions about Jack that were firing around in his brain.

Playing with the dog and chatting with Shane and Mike was a welcome distraction until Ryan called them all into the enormous kitchen. There, Gabe sat between his two best friends at the head of the table while the rest of the family filed in and claimed seats.

After the chaos of finding drinks for everyone and settling the dog with a chew toy, Austin stood and raised his glass.

"To Gabe. Happy Birthday. Hope this year is your best one yet."

"To Gabe!" A chorus of voices echoed, then glasses clinked, and all eyes turned to him once again.

Swallowing his sip of beer, he glanced at each face, over-whelmed in the very best way. Ryan's offer of dinner had been only an hour earlier. The fact that he and Austin had put all of this together at the last minute, and had gotten everyone together, and that they'd all came... He laid a hand on Austin and Ryan's arms. "Thank you all for being here. I know it was short notice. I don't know what to say, except that I'm grateful for all of you."

"You're part of the family, Gabriel." Mike was seated at the other end of the table, but the warmth in his words reached all the way to Gabe's heart. "Now, let's eat."

During a meal of chicken stir fry with wild rice, the family kept Gabe in the center of their attention. The laughter and conversation warmed him as much as the food. He talked books with Leo and gave the hockey player some recommen-dations to share with his teammates who had formed a book club. Then chatted about baseball with Mike and Everson. Then got engrossed in a conversation with Xavier and Kelsey about dog care, even though he hadn't had a dog in years. Through it all, Ryan and Austin kept telling "Gabe stories," their favorite memories, most of which had everyone around the table laughing.

After the meal, there were birthday cards and presents and of course, cake. Two layers of chocolate separated by a layer of caramel frosting and decorated with a pattern of stars dusted across the cake's top with confectioner's sugar.

Chocolate reminded him of Jack, and the cake they'd shared at the bakery. The disappointment that he hadn't heard from the writer and that the writer wasn't there in the room sliced through his gut.

He refocused on the group of people he loved like family and pushed the thoughts of Jack to the back of his mind.

But just like a horror novel killer, the thoughts couldn't be escaped, no matter how hard he tried.

The Saturday evening crowd filling the bar around the corner from Gabe's house added more noise and levity to his ongoing birthday celebration.

Sitting at a high top table, surrounded by Ryan, Austin, Sebastian, Shane, and a few people from the gym and their softball team, he downed a shot—one of the several that people had bought him—and winced at the burn.

The birthday celebration had been Ryan's idea. "Just a casual get-together with some of our buddies," he'd said.

Ryan and Austin had been texting him more frequently over the last few days. They'd avoided bringing up Jack directly, but their subtle questions were enough of an indication that they were concerned.

Gabe was sure they thought he was a mess. He still hadn't heard from the writer, was all but certain that he'd scared the man away.

Dinner with Austin and Ryan at a new Mexican place he'd been dying to try, and now sharing drinks with the rest of their friends at the bar, all of the *Happy Birthdays*, well wishes, and celebrating had gone a long way to raising his spirits.

"Almost the whole team is here," someone behind him said. "Where's Jack? He and Gabe were attached at the hip during our last game."

One of the newer player replied, "I don't see him. Did Ryan invite him? Are he and Gabe together now?"

Shots number two and three slid down like liquid fire, and Gabe welcomed the burn. A physical ache to match his emotional one. He pushed back his chair and wandered away from the group and the questions and speculations. His gaze landed on a couple kissing in the back corner. The men only had eyes for each other. It was sweet and stabbed him in the gut.

Turning away, he banged into Ryan. "Sorry."

"Dude." Ryan wrapped a supporting arm around his shoulders. "You look like you just lost your best friend, which can't be true because I'm right here."

Dredging up a smile was impossible. "Did you invite Jack when you invited everyone else tonight?"

Ryan averted his gaze to somewhere over Gabe's shoulder. "Why don't I get you some water?"

"Ry?"

"Or maybe another drink. Want something to eat?"

"Ryan." Losing patience, he grabbed hold of his friend's arm. "Did you?"

Solemn blue eyes met his gaze. "Yes. Are you mad?"

"What did he say?"

Pursing his lips, Ryan shook his head and then shrugged. "No response."

"Oh." The ache in his gut worsened. He headed back to their table. Downing shot number four helped.

"Have you heard from him yet?" Ryan's voice was gentle as he claimed the stool beside Gabe.

"No."

"Do you want to talk about it?"

"No." But then, suddenly, he did. Or the alcohol did. *Truth serum, at work.* "I think Jack's amazing. Things were going great. Until I sent those texts. Maybe it was too soon to ask him. You know how people can get weird about birthdays and holidays so early on in a relationship… Or whatever this thing is. But it's making me crazy."

When his fingers closed around shot number five, happily purchased by Austin, a firm hand clamped onto his shoulder. He glanced up and into Shane's face. "Hey."

His stand-in older brother frowned, the faint lines on his face etched in concern. "Why are you the only one here who looks like he's not having fun?"

Gabe immediately pasted on a smile. "Oh, I'm fine—"

"He is *not* fine," Ryan's eyes glittered as he snapped out the words. "He hasn't heard from Jack all week. You know that Jack didn't respond to my text, and I know that you haven't heard from him either. Your buddy has pulled another disappearing act."

With a heavy sigh, Shane set his beer down. The corners of his eyes turned down, and he shook his head as he patted Gabe on the back. He dragged a barstool over from another table and sat, lips drawn into a flat line. "Look, he does this when he's writing. Doesn't like to be disturbed. Goes radio silent."

He blinked at Shane as the words settled in. "Who does that? Who just shuts out the world? What if someone needs them?"

"I don't know what to tell you. It's been his process for years."

"Well, it sucks." Gabe slumped in his seat. His stomach clenched into a tight ball as disbelief danced a duet with disappointment. He downed the shot and welcomed the burn. The glass met the table with a bang. "All week long, I've been on edge. Wondering if I scared him off when I asked him to spend part of my birthday with me."

Shane exchanged a glance with Ryan, then he carefully set his beer down and turned his full attention on Gabe. "What did he say when you asked him?"

"It was in a text. He didn't respond."

Firm lines formed into a scowl as Shane's expression darkened. He could look downright scary at times. Gabe swallowed hard. He wouldn't want to be on the receiving end of Shane's ire. "I'll talk to him."

"No." The word shot out, spiked by adrenaline and the desperation to save face. "Don't. Please. I don't want to make things even more awkward."

Lips pressed together, Shane studied him, and then exchanged another one of those looks with Ryan. After a long moment, he dragged his hand through his hair. "It's tough being in the middle."

Wincing, Gabe scrubbed a hand over his face. One look at Shane, and then at Ryan, and a knot formed in his stomach. "I'm sorry."

"Don't be. I love Jack, but sometimes, he can drive me crazy."

Gabe shifted as an uncomfortable thought rolled into his mind. "I don't know what to expect from him at tomorrow's softball game."

Dark storm clouds rolled across Ryan's face, and his hands closed into fists. "I do. I'm going to kick his ass."

"Ry." In spite of himself, Gabe smiled. "You will not. You're not a violent person at all. But thanks for the thought. I know you always have my back."

"I do."

Leaning across the table, Shane held Gabe's gaze. "For what it's worth, I do, too."

"Thanks, guys." He sat back as Austin and several others from their group gathered around the table once again with a fresh round of drinks. Someone asked Shane about Jack's whereabouts, and he didn't miss a beat, telling the group that Jack was writing against a deadline.

Gabe welcomed Ryan's comforting pat on the shoulder. The fact that Jack blocked out the world for extended periods bothered him. Being ignored and shut out never felt good.

If he and Jack were fine, then they'd need an honest conversation about how to better handle that disappearing aspect when Jack finally surfaced. If they weren't fine, and his worries about scaring Jack off were real, then the next time they saw each other was sure to be awkward. Either way, the softball game was at noon the following day. He pulled out his phone to check the time. Midnight. Which meant he'd have his answer in about twelve hours.

Twelve hours to play out every imaginable scenario possible so he could be prepared, because Jack, *damn him*, had somehow worked his way into Gabriel's heart.

CHAPTER TEN

Jack's days flowed between writing and sleeping. More writing than anything else. Time ceased to exist as he lost himself in the world of his own creation. Page after page, chapter after chapter, poured out of him, giving life to the story playing out in his head.

Finally, he reached the end of the draft. Exhaustion claimed him, and he stumbled to bed and dreamed of monsters yet to be revealed.

When he woke, after the first solid block of sleep he'd had in days, he lay in the cool sheets, staring at the ceiling in the darkened room. Faint beams of light gleamed from the perimeter of the windows, creating pale rectangles around the blackout curtains. He couldn't tell the time of day. Birds were chirping, but then again, they usually were. His hand brushed the volume of poetry that he now kept under his pillow. Every time he touched it, he thought of Gabriel.

Gabriel.

Dark haired, blue-eyed Gabriel. Smart and sexy Gabriel. His Gabriel. The urge to see him, to hear his voice, to touch him, was overwhelming.

Pangs of hunger and a rumbling stomach drove him from his bed. Jack padded down the stairs and opened one of the living room curtains, letting light into the space for the first time in… Wait… What day was it?

Scratching his head, he looked for his phone and found it on the bookshelf. He turned it on. The date and time popped up. Sunday, 1pm.

Sunday? He shook his head. How was it already Sunday? And 1pm? That meant he'd slept through the 12pm softball game.

Shit. Shit. Shit.

Notifications of missed calls, voice mails, and texts filled his screen. He thumbed through the texts.

The most recent were from earlier that morning, from Shane.

Shane, 11:50am: Where are you? Game starts in ten minutes. We're short, so if you're not here, we'll have to forfeit.

Shane, 8:30am: Don't forget, we have a game today.

And from earlier in the week, on Wednesday:

Shane, 9pm: Gabe said you're writing, hope it's flowing for you. By the way, it's his birthday today.

Ryan Brennan, 3pm: We're taking Gabe out for his birthday on Saturday night. Meeting up for dinner at 7:00, and then heading out to the bar around the corner from his house. Hope you can join us. I know he'd like you to be there.

And from Tuesday:

Gabriel, 10am: Hey, I wasn't sure if I should say anything since this thing with us is new, and holidays or special occasions so early on can make things weird, but my birthday is tomorrow. Want to celebrate, just you and me? Birthday cake for dinner, and each other for dessert? :-) Let me know.

And from Monday:

Gabriel, 8am: Just wanted to say I was thinking of you. I hope the writing is going well.

Shit.

He'd missed Gabe's birthday. And the birthday celebration with friends. And the softball game.

Damn. It.

He was a shit friend and an even shittier boyfriend, or whatever it was that he and Gabe were to each other. Shane had complained a few times in the past about Jack going off the grid when writing, but he hadn't realized how much of an inconsiderate jerk checking out of everything made him, until now.

And Gabriel's message… It looked awful that Jack hadn't responded. Maybe Gabe's phone could tell that the messages hadn't been read. Stomach in knots, he dialed Gabriel's number and paced the floor. He caught his reflection in the mirror. His hair stuck out in all directions, his T-shirt and sweats were rumpled, and he was in desperate need of a shave.

One ring turned into two, then three, then four, then five. Just as he thought he'd have to leave a voice mail, Gabriel's voice came through the speaker. "Hey."

"I'm sorry I missed your birthday." He blurted out the words in a rush. "I've had my phone turned off since I got home on Monday morning."

"Yeah. Shane said you do that." Gabe's tone was flat, devoid of all emotion.

Shit. He needed to talk and talk fast. Devoid of all emotion might translate to Gabe being over and done with the entire situation. He couldn't let that happen. "Look, I didn't realize how much time had passed. I was writing and in the zone. The words were flowing. I couldn't stop. And except for sleeping, I didn't."

"You at least remembered to eat, though, right?"

"I did." Handfuls of jelly beans, chocolate drops, and copious amounts of coffee. He knew Gabriel wouldn't have approved.

"Oh. Well, good." Gabe's tone hadn't changed, but at least he was still on the phone. That was a good sign, right? Music, murmurs of conversations, and clanking glasses flowed from the speaker, filling the silence.

Jack latched onto the noise. "Are you at the bar with the team? Does that mean you won the game? You found someone to fill in for me?"

"We couldn't get anyone who could show up quick enough. It sucked to have to forfeit. I know we're all about fun, but we still look forward to playing the game."

"I'm sorry." The words couldn't convey how much he meant it. He rubbed his hand over the heaviness in his chest. "I'm probably on Shane's shit list right now. He said last week that if we won today's game and next week's game, that we could make the playoffs. That can't happen now, thanks to me."

"It's not just you. Austin was too sick to play. He was hungover from last night."

"I'm sorry I missed that birthday celebration too."

"Hey, I get it. Work comes first. It's cool."

It wasn't cool. Not when the words were delivered in a muted, disappointed tone that was straining to sound brighter and happier. Jack dragged his hand through his hair. "I admit, the words can consume me, but from now on, I'll be better about checking my phone and checking in. How long do you think you'll be at the bar?"

"I'm not sure about the rest of the team, but I'm leaving now. I need to do laundry and get caught up on some things before work tomorrow."

No invitation to join him or for them to get together. Was he truly just busy and tired, or angry and disappointed and wanting no parts of Jack? "Can I call you later?"

"If you want."

The call ended, but not before he heard someone call out Gabriel's name. Someone unfamiliar. Maybe someone who wouldn't ghost out of his life for an entire week. Jack glared at his reflection. He had to make it up to the man. But how?

Inspiration struck as he headed toward the kitchen. While his coffee brewed, he searched food blogs for an easy cake recipe. A trip to the grocery store was in order. So was a shower. And a meal more substantial than the candy he'd consumed during the week.

Fresh energy let him knock out the trip to the store and he confidently threw himself into lining up ingredients. Following a recipe would be easy. After all, it was only following directions. How hard could that be?

———

The doorbell chimed, accompanied by someone pounding on his door, wrenching Jack from staring at the epic disaster in front of him. He'd been at it for two hours, was wearing more batter than was in the newly purchased pans, and was ready to admit defeat.

Could it be Gabe? Heartbeat racing, Jack grabbed a towel to wipe his hands. His elbow hit the bag of sugar, and it fell, scattering an avalanche of white grains across the table and onto the floor.

"Damn it." He abandoned the mess and rushed to the front door. Through the beveled glass, he made out Shane and Ryan standing on the other side.

Shit. He'd been so caught up in the cake that he'd never

called or texted Shane. Yanking the door open, he readied his apology, but neither Ryan's thunderous expression nor Shane's blank mask seemed receptive.

Shane raised a brow and scanned Jack from his head to his toes. "Just checking to make sure you're still alive."

"I'm sorry about missing the game." He stepped back, gesturing for them to enter, relieved when they passed through the door and didn't simply walk away. "I let you down. I know you guys said you don't like it when I turn my phone off. I finally understand. I promise I'll be more considerate in the future. You have every right to be pissed off."

A long expulsion of breath left Shane's lips. He dipped his hands into his pockets and rocked back on his heels. "I'm not angry."

"I am," Ryan stepped in front of his brother, hands curled into fists and fire in his gaze. "And not only about the game and ghosting us. You missed Gabe's birthday."

"I know. I'm sorry."

"He really likes you. I thought you liked him too."

"I do."

Ryan advanced on him, invading Jack's personal space. The looming move mimicked memories of schoolyard and neighborhood bullies, and Jack flinched.

Shane clamped a hand on Ryan's shoulder and yanked his brother back.

Stumbling, Ryan glanced at Shane and then at Jack and took a breath. "Sorry…" his voice gentled. "Gabe's been thinking all week that he scared you away by asking you to hang out and celebrate his birthday with him."

"Well, he didn't. I got caught up writing."

"We figured as much. We're used to that, and we told him that was probably the reason, but he isn't used to your disappearing act." Disapproval dripped from his words.

Jack winced. He'd thought he couldn't feel any worse. He'd been wrong. He gestured at the streaks of flour and sugar and batter on his clothes. "I'm trying to bake him a cake to make up for it."

Ryan looked past him to peer into the kitchen. He eyed the misshapen mess on the kitchen table and did a double-take. "You can't give him *that*."

"No kidding." Glaring at the disaster he'd created wouldn't make it better. Ryan was his only hope. "Help me, please?"

A raised eyebrow, a measured glance, and then finally, a single nod. "Fine. But you have to make some changes, Jack. My brother shouldn't have to wonder whether days of silence mean you're writing or if you're dead."

"Ry…" With a quelling look, Shane shifted closer to his brother.

Ryan's hand shot up, waving off Shane's warning. "No. Remember how you found Jack passed out on his bedroom floor when he had the flu last year? That followed a week of no contact too. Jack, you freaked him the hell out back then, not that he'd ever tell you how scared he'd been when he found you. Assuming the worst with you lying there, motion-less. Every time you go for days without contact, people worry."

Jack blinked at Ryan. Guilt tripled in weight as he turned toward Shane. "Words are meaningless unless backed up by actions, but the words still need to be said. I'm sorry. I promise I'll be better. I mean it."

Shane held his gaze, but other than a slight lifting of his brows, his expression had returned to carefully blank. "Okay."

"I'll set an alarm to text or call you every day if that helps."

His best friend's lips finally creased into a smile. "You don't have to go that far."

"Alarms don't work if you turn your phone off, though." Ryan's words, rough and blunt, ripped into Jack's hopeful resolve. The youngest Brennan brother could be just as protective as Shane when it came to people he cared about, and with this, he was like a dog gnawing at a bone.

"Ryan, I get it." Jack spoke at the same time as Shane said, "Ry, let it go."

Ryan held up his hands and backed into the kitchen. "Okay, okay, I will. Now let's see about salvaging this cake."

Standing in the heat of the late afternoon sun, holding a bottle of champagne and a tray of freshly baked brownies he and Ryan had baked, Jack knocked on Gabriel's door.

It opened halfway, and Gabe stood before him in a light blue T-shirt that matched his eyes and light gray workout shorts. He smelled like fabric softener and cookies. But his smile was hesitant and his gaze unsure. "Hi."

Guilt stabbed his gut. He'd dimmed Gabriel's shine, and that was unforgivable. Jack held up the champagne and brownies. "Happy belated Birthday."

Gabriel's brows lifted, his eyes widened, and his lips curved in the most beautiful smile. "Thank you."

The tension in Jack's stomach eased. "Better late than never."

"Come in." Gabe pushed the door open wider, revealing the cozy living room and a refreshing blast of air-conditioned air. "How's the book coming?"

"I finished the draft. I'll get started on my second pass of the manuscript tomorrow." He paused in front of the coffee table. "Where should I set this down?"

"The kitchen. I'll get glasses."

Four birthday cards lined the kitchen counter, one from Ashley and Xavier, one from Austin, one from Ryan and Everson, and one signed by the rest of the Brennans. Jack set the brownies beside the colorful cards. "In the interest of full disclosure, Ryan helped me bake this. I tried making a cake on my own, and it was a disaster. Cake batter got everywhere, and I must have screwed something up because it was both over-baked and underdone."

Laughing, Gabe took two champagne flutes from the cabinet. "It was sweet that you tried."

Jack had to touch him, had to make sure they were really okay and that Gabe understood how sorry he was. He laid his hands on Gabe's shoulders. "I'm sorry I missed celebrating your birthday with you, and I'm sorry I didn't see the messages."

Faint shadows under his eyes emphasized the vulnerability in Gabe's gaze. "I thought I made things weird by telling you about my birthday."

"No. Far from it." Jack caressed his shoulders and then forced himself to step back. Gabe deserved a distraction-free apology. "When I'm writing, I don't want anything to interrupt the flow, so I turn off my phone and unplug my alarm clock, and basically do everything I can to make sure I won't be disturbed."

Some of the light in his gaze dimmed once again. "Shane and Ryan told me some stories last night. I still don't see how you can tune out the entire world like that."

Regret swarmed in, uncomfortable and overwhelming. "I knew it bugged some people, but it's always been how I've done things. I finally realize I can't do that anymore. Like I said on the phone, I promise I'll be better about checking in and communicating." Earnestness made his words come quicker. "I know talk is one thing. Only time will show you if I'm really going to follow through. I hope you'll give me the chance."

Gabe nodded and toyed with one of the glasses, his gaze focused on the shining crystal. "I don't want to be an annoyance."

"You're not. You couldn't be." Desperate to fix things, he took hold of the glass and set it aside and then grabbed Gabe's hand, willing Gabe to believe him. "I think you're amazing."

Blue eyes widened and shifted from the darkness of doubt to lightened with hope. His gaze clung to Jack's, and his fingers curled tight around Jack's hand, locking them together. "Really?"

With two steps, Jack closed the small distance between them. He pressed a soft kiss to Gabe's lips, and his heartbeat stuttered like an engine starting after a long lull. The feel and scent and taste of Gabriel revived him, and he craved more. Slanting his mouth, he coaxed and teased and delved deeper. His hands grabbed fistfuls of Gabe's shirt and then roamed over his torso roughened by want and desire and need.

A sigh turned into a groan, and Gabe melted against him. Strong arms curled around Jack's back, and his fingers flexed and released and flexed and released, sealing him in strength and security. When Jack lifted his head, Gabe ran his fingers along the sides of Jack's face and into his hair, keeping him close. His mouth curled into a gentle smile. Something shifted and settled deep in Jack's core, and he slid his arms around Gabe's waist, content to simply hold him.

He wasn't sure how long they stood together like that, but he could spend an eternity wrapped up in Gabriel.

Finally, Gabe pulled away with a shaky breath. "How about some brownies and champagne?"

"Sure." More settled, Jack sliced into the dessert and dished up two large squares while Gabe opened the bottle and filled the flutes. He wasn't sure if they were still on shaky ground, but Gabe's smile went a long way to easing his mind.

He raised his glass. "Happy Birthday, Gabriel."

Cheeks flushed, Gabe clinked their glasses together. "Thank you."

The champagne bubbled on his tongue, frothy and light like the tingles of happiness sparking throughout his body.

Jack set the glass aside and then broke off a piece of brownie and held it to Gabe's lips. Gabe's mouth closed over the bite, and his tongue swiped over the tips of Jack's fingers. Then Gabe returned the favor, feeding Jack a taste.

After swallowing the decadent chocolate, Jack wrapped his hand around Gabe's wrist and pressed a kiss to his palm. "What were you going to do tonight? Am I interrupting anything?"

"I'm all done with what I needed to do. Laundry and bills and cleaning are finished, so I can relax for the rest of the night. There's a new bake-off show on at nine. Rival bakers from the same city are facing off. It should be good." His smile turned shy. "Want to stay and watch it with me?"

"I do." He caressed Gabe's cheek, loving how the soft beard felt against his hand. "So, we're okay?"

"We're okay, Jack." Gabriel kissed him again, and relief was as sweet as the chocolate. He eased back, a smile on his lips, and brushed his hand down the center of Jack's chest. "If you're starting on the second draft of your book tomorrow, you'll need fuel to write. I promised you cookies."

"You don't have to do that. Especially not tonight. Considering how I messed up, I don't expect cookies at all."

"A promise is a promise." Gabe's gaze dropped to the brownie, and his voice lowered to an almost murmur, "Maybe when you see them, you'll think of me."

Jack took hold of Gabe's hips and shifted until he'd caged Gabe against the counter. "Gabriel. I don't need a cookie to do that. You're the first thing I thought of when I came up for air. The very first thing."

Gabe's parted lips were so close, and so needing Jack's kiss if any doubt still lingered in his mind. "I…"

Framing Gabe's face with his hands, Jack leaned in, inch by inch, watching as Gabe's eyes closed. And then he kissed him. Long and slow and so very sweet, pouring all of his apology into the meeting of their lips.

Gabriel raised his head and gazed into Jack's eyes. Something soft and new shimmered in the blue depths. "You definitely deserve cookies."

"You don't have to—"

"I want to do it. Please. We can bake them together."

"Then I'll buy dinner. It's the least I can do. What do you want?"

"You decide. You're the guest."

"No." In this, Jack would be firm. "Tonight is a do-over of your birthday. You pick."

That sweet smile, combined with the pleasure lighting over Gabe's face, as though Jack had offered something unexpected, would undo him. "Honestly? I just want spaghetti."

"Then that's what we'll have." Jack directed Gabe to a seat at the table and then brought over their glasses and plates. "What did you do on your birthday?"

"I worked, then went to the gym, then had dinner at Ryan's. His whole family was there."

Jack glanced at the birthday cards again. There wasn't

anything from Gabriel's family. Ryan had mentioned while they were baking that Gabe had spoken to his parents on his special day and that the conversation had been stilted at best and had left Gabe feeling sad. Getting angry on Gabe's behalf wouldn't solve anything, but he would do anything he could to make up for it. "Again, I'm sorry I wasn't there. You had a good time with the Brennans?"

"I did." Gabe ate another bite of brownie. "So, you finished the draft of the book. Were the things I showed you at the bakery helpful?"

"Absolutely. I… Do you want to hear about the book?"

"Sure. I'm curious about how Horror Gabe is doing."

Laughing, Jack managed to swallow his champagne without choking. "Well, first off, just so we're clear, Horror Gabe is *not* you. Yes, he's a baker, and he's super nice, has some of your mannerisms, and he does have a library. I think you'd like it. Books are everywhere, from floor to ceiling. Anyway, that's where the similarities end. Horror Gabe, who, by the way, is *not* named Gabe or Gabriel, takes out some pretty awful guys at first, so I hope the readers will be almost rooting for him."

"Like a vigilant?"

"In his mind, yes. He uses the bakery and some of the baking equipment to settle some, um, unfinished and messy business. And the delivery van is working out perfectly for him to accomplish some necessary evil too. Let's just say his tool bag for emergencies is a lot lighter on the piping bags and a lot heavier on the sharp objects."

"Oh no." Gabe gave an exaggerated shudder, but his eyes were twinkling and his tone was light. "Maybe in your next book, the good guy can be a baker. You know, to kind of redeem the profession."

"Or, maybe in my next book, the hero can be not a fan of

horror at all, like *someone* I know," Jack captured Gabe's hand and raised it to his lips for a kiss.

Smiling, Gabe laced their fingers together. "Now that's the kind of character I can see myself inspiring."

"And then he finds himself essentially starring in his own worst nightmare."

Gabe's eyes closed for a moment as he shuddered again. "That *would* be my worst nightmare."

Sparks of an idea were popping off like fireworks. Jack broke away and yanked out his phone. Fingers flew over the keypad, racing to keep up with his thoughts. Gabe as a star of his book again, but this time, as a hero. Another plot was coming to life, but he had a real-life hero sitting before him, and that one needed and deserved his full attention.

He saved the memo and set the phone on the opposite side of the table, nearly out of reach. "Sorry about that, but I've learned the hard way that if I don't write ideas down immediately, they can disappear for good."

"No worries. I just thought of another hero idea. Make him a writer who does battle, just so you can work in that *pen is mightier than the sword* line."

Jack burst out laughing. "I love it. My editor will too."

Leaning back in his chair, Gabe sipped his champagne. "You look cute when you're writing away in your notebook."

"You should've seen me the past few days. I doubt you'd have thought that a severe case of bed head, wrinkled clothes, and dark circles were cute."

"Hmm." The brightness in his eyes matched the brightness of his smile as Gabe stroked a hand over his beard. "Maybe I should add notes to your cookies. But instead of *Nice Try*, *Home Run*, and *All-Star*, it would be *Drink Water, Get Some Sleep,* and *Eat Something.*"

The idea warmed him. Jack lifted a shoulder but held

back from saying that just having cookies made especially for him would be enough, even though it was true. He'd gladly take any extra attention and care that Gabriel wanted to give him. "Reminders couldn't hurt."

"I liked you with bed head the other morning." Gabe's voice dropped, and he shifted his chair closer and brushed his fingers along Jack's cheek. "All rumpled from sleeping in my bed."

Desire flared as bright and hot as a sunburst. "Is that an invitation for me to stay over tonight?"

"Want to?"

"I do." He stood and pulled Gabe to his feet. But before he could draw the man into another kiss, Gabe pressed a finger to Jack's lips.

"Wait. We need to start the cookies." He preheated the oven and pulled sticks of butter and two eggs from the fridge. Bustling around Jack with natural grace, he opened cabinets and drawers and took out bowls and utensils. Within minutes, he had several ingredients lining the counter.

Jack leaned along the counter's edge. "Tell me what to do and how to do it."

"First, we're creaming the butter and sugars." Gabe had him measure out the amounts of brown and granulated sugars and add them to the mixing bowl. Together, they added the eggs and vanilla, and then the dry ingredients, including the cocoa powder and instant coffee granules, in a separate bowl.

Next, Gabe slowly added the dry ingredient mixture into the wet ingredients. Jack came up behind him and slid his arms around Gabe's waist. Resting his chin on Gabe's shoulder, he covered Gabe's hand as it stirred the batter. "I'm helping."

Gabe let out a breath and leaned against Jack. "I like your help."

"Here's more." Jack kissed his neck, trailing from one side to the other. "How's that?"

"Good. Really good." Gabe's hand shook as he sprinkled a cup of chocolate chips into the bowl. Jack gently brushed his hand aside and took over, stirring in the chips.

"What now?"

"Now, we scoop them onto the baking sheet." Gabe demonstrated with the medium-sized cookie scoop from his collection of baking tools. "They need to be evenly spaced. Can you press extra chocolate chips into the tops?"

Jack followed along, adding chips to each cookie, making sure to touch Gabe with every movement. "Are they ready to go in?"

In two smooth moves, Gabe slid the two trays into the oven. "They'll only take ten to twelve minutes."

Jack waited until the timer was set. "That's just enough time."

"For what?"

"This." Capturing Gabe's lips, he backed Gabe into the counter. His hands traveled up and down and finally under Gabe's T-shirt, roaming over the dips and planes of hard muscle and soft skin.

His body craved Gabe's, tingling everywhere Gabe touched him, from the hands in his hair to the hard torso pressed against his own. Needing more, Jack continued his exploration, journeying lower, tracing a path down Gabe's happy trail, and Gabe's stomach sucked in, tightening with his sharp intake of breath.

Jack kissed his way down Gabe's neck, then, holding his gaze, he sank to his knees. Hooking his fingers into the waist-band of Gabe's shorts, he lowered the material down narrow hips. Eyes half-mast, Gabe grasped the counter and widened his stance.

Nodding and smiling in approval, Jack drew the workout shorts and Gabe's boxers down his legs. Gabe's cock sprang free, hard and wet, and Jack didn't make him wait. He stroked and kissed and laved and sucked in alternating speeds, slow then fast, hard then soft, using Gabe's moans and whimpers and gasps as a guide.

The timer's countdown continued, and Jack's game of beat the clock took on more urgency with each passing second. At the one minute mark, he poured on the power, fast and hard, lingering on the spots that made Gabe cry out.

Fingers tightened in his hair, pulling Jack closer as Gabe's hips thrust deeper. That hitch of breath meant Gabe was close. Jack swallowed him down and palmed his ass, kneading and squeezing until Gabe stiffened and clutched Jack to him as he groaned through his release.

The hold on his curls gentled and turned into a caress. Jack eased back, kissing and licking, and listening to Gabe's breathing return to normal.

Beep. Beep. Beep. Beep.

The timer intruded on the quiet moment.

Jack sat back on his heels and grinned at Gabe. "See? Just enough time."

One hand left the counter and reached for him. "Come here."

He pulled Gabe's clothes back in place as he rose, and as soon as he was heart to heart, Gabe cupped his cheek and drew him into a kiss.

Beep. Beep. Beep. Beep.

"I've got it." Jack donned the oven mitts and removed the trays of chocolate-scented goodness from the oven. Twenty perfect cookies in four perfect lines, courtesy of Gabe's handiwork.

Gabe roused himself from the counter and dug out

cooling racks from a low cabinet. "We can leave the cookies on the trays for now. They need a few minutes there before we move them to the cooling racks."

"Then we can start making dinner now."

"Dinner can wait a minute." Gaze darkened with desire, Gabe removed the oven mitts from Jack's hands one at a time. He tossed them onto the counter and drew Jack into his arms. "First, this…"

Firm lips settled over Jack's, and then Gabe's tongue traced the seam of Jack's mouth. Jack moaned when he slipped inside. Gabe's hands were hot and restless and *everywhere*, turning Jack into a pile of need.

Sure, seeking hands ripped away his control, diving deep as they stroked in time with the thrusts of his tongue. He slipped his leg between Jack's and encouraged him to grind, and all of the motions—hands, hips, and lips—worked together to send him over the edge.

His release coated Gabe's hand and landed on his shirt and completely addled his brain. He gazed at Gabe, lost in his kisses, safe in his embrace, as reality slid back into place.

Gabe grinned at him. "Now, we can make dinner."

They leaned into each other, trading kisses as they cleaned up the kitchen and waited for the spaghetti to cook. The touching continued while they ate the simple meal, and Jack hoped it would continue all night long.

As he settled on the couch, ready to watch the bake-off show with Gabriel, his phone screen lit up with an email notification. He was lucky he'd turned his phone on that afternoon. If the draft had taken extra days, he might have been conspicuously absent from yet another event. "Sorry, I just need to respond to this message. It won't take long."

Gabe set two glasses of champagne on the coffee table. "Is everything okay?"

Angling the phone screen, he showed Gabe the message. "I have a book signing on Tuesday night at the bookstore on Passyunk Avenue. I'd forgotten about it."

"Sounds like fun." Gabe eased onto the cushion beside him and picked up one of the glasses. "That's a nice bookstore too."

It would be even nicer to have Gabriel there with him. "Do you want to come and keep me company?"

Gabe paused with his glass halfway to his lips. Something flickered across his face too quickly for Jack to name. "Will I be in the way?"

He pressed a kiss to Gabe's temple. "No. I always worry that no readers will show up. And to be honest, crowds can make me nervous. If you're sitting with me, it'll help."

"Then I'll be there," Gabe promised. Just like that. He'd be there. He'd help. Simply because Jack had asked.

Jack finished typing his response, then set his phone on silent and pulled Gabe into his arms. Gabe snuggled in closer, his head a welcome weight on Jack's shoulder. Stroking his hand through the thick richness of Gabe's hair, he settled against the couch as the baking competition got underway on the TV and listened to Gabe's explanation of the show.

He didn't deserve the man. But tonight, he hoped that he'd shown Gabe how sorry he was, and how much Gabe mattered. Gabriel was quickly becoming someone important, vital even, in Jack's life. His feelings were running deeper, further, and faster than with anyone else.

Hopefully, he wouldn't do anything else stupid to mess up the relationship.

CHAPTER ELEVEN

A rumble of thunder filled his ears as Gabriel emerged from the subway station. He glanced at the dark, ominous gray sky and waited for the crack of lightning. *It was a dark and stormy night.* He laughed at himself as the line sprang into his thoughts. The weather was perfect for an evening about horror novels. Fat raindrops splashed his face as he hurried the few blocks to the bookstore.

He tucked the bakery box closer to his chest. Ashley hadn't minded him staying late at the shop to make the treats. Hopefully, Jack would like them.

The bright lights of the bookstore welcomed him in, as did the scent of coffee and the numerous shelves of books. He'd visited the shop often when he'd first moved to Philly, taking refuge there every time loneliness had overwhelmed him. Books had always been a comfort and an escape.

Jack waved from a table in the back of the room. The area that usually held comfortable chairs meant for settling in had been reconfigured to showcase Jack right in the center.

Dressed in a dark button-down shirt and faded jeans that accentuated his lanky form, he stood as Gabe got closer. He'd gotten a haircut sometime within the two days since Gabe had seen him last, the soft curls artfully framed his face, and probably some sleep given the lack of shadows under his eyes. Fresh, polished, and utterly edible, he smiled and rounded the table. "Thanks for coming."

"Sure." Gabe set the box on an empty spot next to a small stack of Jack's latest novel and then rubbed at the raindrops on his skin. "Here. I brought cookies, but you don't have to put them out."

Jack winked at him. "I always want your cookies."

Nerves pricked his stomach as Jack opened the box. The sugar cookies were decorated to match the cover of the book. Hand-piping all of the details had taken the better part of two hours. The muscles in his forearms were still sore.

"I can't believe you did this for me." Voice soft and eyes wide, Jack picked up one of the cookies. "Saying thank you isn't nearly enough, but thank you. They're amazing."

"You like them?"

"They're too nice to eat." He pulled out his phone and took a few photos of the treats. "I'll post this now. The weather might deter people from coming out, but if anything will draw them here, it's these cookies."

Gabe's phone went off a few moments later. Jack had tagged both him and the bakery in the post. The publicity would be good, not that the bakery needed too much help there. New custom orders kept flowing in, and the stream of repeat and new customers continued to climb. Ashley had mentioned again, while they were elbow-deep in cake batter, that she needed to hire more help, at least another assistant, and someone else to help out at the front counter and with deliveries.

He pocketed his phone and turned his attention to Jack. "What can I do to help?"

Jack leaned in and cupped Gabe's face in his hands. "For starters, this."

The kiss was light, but Gabe felt it all the way to his toes. Jack tasted like coffee and mint. And the way his thumb stroked Gabe's cheek, slowly, so slowly, like Gabe was something to be treasured, weakened him. He held Jack's shoulders, reluctant to draw away.

Voices rang out from the store's front end, and the click of heels on hardwood grew louder. Gabe slowly lifted his head. The shop's owner approached them. "Mr. Kramer, if you need anything, just let me know. We're ready to get started."

Jack nodded and rounded the table and motioned for Gabe to sit beside him. As Gabe settled in, he laid his hand on Jack's thigh in support and squeezed. For all of Jack's concern about the weather keeping people away, he needn't have worried. People were lining up, waiting for their chance to meet him.

Jack greeted the first readers who arrived by name. As they chatted, Gabe gathered that they'd attended Jack's previous signings. More people came, and Jack signed the books and posed for pictures and told every single person that Gabe had made the cookies.

Gabe ran out of the small stack of business cards he carried for the bakery, and when the conversation shifted to the latest horror movie remake to hit the big screen, he ran out of conversation too.

But Jack was in his element. He enthused about the plot and the changes and dove into an in-depth discussion about comparisons to the original. The original, which Gabe hadn't been able to handle the night that Jack had come over. He chided himself for being such a baby, as everyone else was chiming in, and he sat there with nothing to contribute. As the minutes ticked by and more gore and lore were discussed, he felt increasingly out of place.

He returned from fetching fresh coffee for Jack and himself at the same moment as a tall, handsome man with a glint of silver at his temples approached the table. He held a well-worn copy of one of Jack's books in his hand. "I'm a huge fan, Jack. It's a thrill to meet you."

Jack stood to shake his hand, and the reader's gaze tracked over his body, lingering too long for Gabe's liking. He set the coffees down with a clatter and took his place at Jack's side. Jack glanced at him and smiled. "Thanks, babe." Then, he looked at the reader and motioned to Gabe. "He made the cookies. Help yourself."

The man spared a glance at Gabe and then at the cookies, and then returned his attention to Jack. "I'd love for you to sign my book. Can you make it out to Curtis?"

"Is that you, or is this a gift for someone else?"

"It's me." Curtis rested his hands on the table and leaned in, gaze steady on Jack as he signed. "I've been devouring your work for years."

Jack finishing scrawling his signature, set his pen down and handed the book over. "I appreciate the support."

"I loved how you did live social media posts during your 80's slasher movie marathon last month. It was like we were right there, watching along with you. It's great to see that you're such a fan of the genre."

Jack grinned. "Glad you liked it. I'm thinking of doing more of those. Maybe the original *Dracula* and all of the remakes for next month."

"You should. I'm a big fan of them too." Curtis held up his phone. "Could I get a photo with you?"

"Sure." Jack rounded the table as he had for the other

photos. He smiled at Gabe and inclined his head. "Thanks for playing photographer tonight."

Gabe nodded and held out his hand for Curtis's phone. Some of the readers had put their arm around Jack for the photos, and some hadn't. Curtis wrapped his arm around Jack and stepped closer, eliminating all space between them. Then, he leaned his head in so that his temple brushed Jack's hair.

Jealousy flared hot and bright, tempting Gabe to *accidentally* drop the guy's phone, or wiggle the camera to ensure a blurry photo, but he didn't give in to either impulse. He took two pictures, then thrust the phone at Curtis, forcing him back a few steps. "Here you go."

Curtis slipped his phone away, and Gabe moved next to Jack once again. He draped an arm over Jack's shoulder, pleased and proud when Jack leaned against him. But as the conversation continued, and Curtis engaged Jack in a barrage of questions and compliments about Jack's latest book, Jack and Curtis seemed to have a lot more in common than Jack and Gabe. He nodded and smiled and pretended to understand all of the premises and theories, but all he could think was how he could lose Jack to that guy.

When a new set of readers approached, relief flooded through Gabe like a burst of cool air on a hot day. He smiled and waved them over, and the jerk monopolizing all of Jack's attention finally got the hint that he should leave.

Curtis shook Jack's hand once again. "I'd love to talk more with you. Want to grab a drink later? There's a great bar two blocks away."

"Thanks, but I can't." Jack slid his arm around Gabe's waist. Gabe let out a breath, relieved, and shifted his hand from Jack's shoulder to the back of his neck.

Gaze flicking between them, Curtis addressed Jack, "You're together?"

Both Jack's hold and his voice firmed. "Yes."

Curtis spared Gabe another glance, and this time, it lingered. "So, which of Jack's books is your favorite?"

"Ah… well…" Shit. Gabe stammered as heat rushed into his cheeks. He cast a desperate glance at the stack of books on the table and the copy in Curtis's hands. He didn't want to admit that he hadn't read the books, especially after nodding and smiling along with everything the guy had been saying about those books, but he couldn't lie because he didn't have any idea about the details of the plots. And, because Jack knew he hadn't read any of them. "It's… It's hard to pick a favorite."

Curtis raised a brow and smirked, as though he saw right through Gabe's lame response. "Right. Well, great meeting you, Jack. I can't wait for the next book. And I look forward to your next signing. Maybe you'll be free, and we can share a drink then."

Gabe watched Curtis walk away. The weight of Jack's hand on his waist should have reassured him, but it didn't. He shifted as embarrassment warred with anger. Who the hell did Curtis think he was?

More people came to the table. And the gushing and praise and talking—about Jack's books, books of other authors in the genre, and movies—started all over again. Gabe sat, smile in place, stewing over the encounter with Curtis. He couldn't get that knowing smirk out of his mind or the thought blaring like a siren that he didn't belong. He desperately wanted to feel more a part of Jack's world.

While Jack greeted a couple wearing shirts with his author logo, Gabe quietly excused himself. The store had all of Jack's titles on a small table by the register. He picked up copies of each and handed them to the cashier. As she rang him up, he glanced at the clock on the wall. Nearly closing time. The longest two hours of his life were almost over. Fresh energy filled him as he returned to the table.

Jack gestured to the bag Gabe carried. "What did you get?"

"Your books. I figure it's time I read them."

Brown eyes lit up, and the most beautiful smile spread across Jack's face. "Really?"

"Will you sign them for me?"

He signed each of them *For Gabriel* and then wrote his signature with a flourish in bold, red ink. "You'll let me know what you think, right?"

"I promise I will. I'll start reading the first book tomorrow."

Finally, the signing ended, and they walked to Jack's car, side-stepping puddles along the way. The rain had stopped and taken the clouds with it. The moon shone full and bright as though everything around them had been washed clean.

Jack laced their fingers together. "Thanks again for being there tonight."

"With the number of people, you didn't end up needing me."

"That's the thing, though." They came to a stop at Jack's car, and instead of reaching for his keys, Jack stepped in front of Gabe and traced his fingers along Gabe's cheek. "I did need you. Just knowing you were there helped calm me down."

"Then I'm glad I could be of service."

Warm fingers crept up Gabe's side, and Jack slid his other hand into Gabe's hair. "I can be of service too. Come home with me?"

His body heated with the promise in Jack's voice, with the knowledge of what those fingers and that mouth could do. He wasn't comfortable *at all* in Jack's house of horrors, but the way Curtis had made him feel, and the *on the outside looking in* feeling he'd had all night were even worse. Frustration at himself firmed his resolve. "Sure."

He could be everything Jack needed.

He damn sure had to try.

CHAPTER TWELVE

Jack arrived at the ball field early for the final game of the season. He sought out the other early arrivals and apologized to them for missing the last game and causing the forfeit. As each teammate arrived, he repeated his words.

No one was mean, but a few weren't as friendly as they'd been before. Gabe's words came back to him about this league being fun, but people still wanted to play. Maybe buying the first round at the bar post-game would help.

Shane hadn't again asked him about joining the Fall league. Perhaps that was for the best. But he'd had more fun than he'd anticipated. If invited back, he'd play again.

He spun in a slow circle, scanning the field for Gabe.

Five days had passed since the night at the bookstore. He'd been busy with the second draft of the book, editing and revising, and savored each of the special *writer fuel* cookies, and had even made it to the gym for his regular late-morning sessions, much to Shane's surprise and happiness. But through it all, he'd thought about Gabe.

And thought it odd that Gabe hadn't responded to the few texts and the one phone call Jack had sent him. Perhaps he was busy at the bakery, and it wasn't like they were on the same schedules. Night owl versus an early riser. But he missed Gabe, and now fully understood how frustrating waiting to hear back from someone could be.

Maybe Gabe hadn't liked his books. For someone who devoured at least a book a week, Gabe seemed like he was taking a long time to read the first one. Not liking them was the only option Jack could think of for Gabe avoiding him.

Nerves lodged like a ball in his stomach. Gabe's opinion mattered. Of course, he wanted Gabe to like them, wanted Gabe to think they were good, wanted Gabe to look at him with pride in his eyes, just as Jack did when Gabe showed him pictures of custom cakes he'd made.

Shouldering his bag, he wandered across the field to set his things in the dugout. What if Gabe wasn't avoiding him, but was merely sick? Had he missed work? Had anyone checked on him? Maybe he should call again.

He'd pulled out his phone, intending to do just that when Shane came in through the break in the fence. Smiling wide, he clasped Jack's hand and used it to pull him into a hug. "Hey. Ready for the last game? By the way, what's your thought on playing with us in the Fall league? I hope you'll play."

"Have you heard from Gabe? I haven't all week."

Shane's eyes narrowed as he scanned the field. "He sent me a text and said he wasn't playing today, and that Sebastian would be taking his place. But I swear I just saw him as I was walking down the block. He's… There. Over by the bleachers."

Jack turned, shading his eyes from the sun.

Gabriel stood by the bleachers of the adjoining ball field, talking with Ryan. He wasn't wearing the team T-shirt. Without another word to Shane, Jack detoured in their direction. Their backs were to him. As he approached, he heard *Jack* and *book* and slowed his pace, straining to hear more, curious for Gabriel's honest opinion.

"All three were gross and terrifying." Voice strained, Gabriel scraped his hands through his hair. "They're... Ry... This is so far beyond my comfort level, I can't even... I'm freaking out. I don't know what the hell to even say to him."

Oh.

His stomach sagged like a lead weight. Jack stopped moving.

"And it's not just the books. His whole house is like a horror memorabilia museum. Do you know what it's like to come face to face with a *Dracula* poster or a *Scream* mask or a *Psycho* shower curtain at two in the morning when you're half-asleep? Fucking terrifying." Pain filled his voice, and he tugged at his shirt and then wrapped his arms around his torso. "I can't ask him to change who he is, Ry. But I can't pretend I'm cool with everything either."

Jack's thoughts grew fuzzy. His heart felt like it was shrinking. He must have made a sound because Ryan and Gabriel turned toward him.

More than the books. So much more than the books. *Everything.*

The distressed, pained expression on Gabriel's face gutted him even more. Jack swallowed hard. The ache in his chest made breathing difficult.

He'd been here before, with other boyfriends and family members. But he'd thought Gabriel was different. No, he'd wanted to believe that Gabe was different. Had believed it.

He cleared his throat, and no doubt failed in his attempt to smile. "I guess we need to talk."

Gabriel stared at Jack, unsure of how to start. All week, he'd wrestled with what to say and how to say it. But worse was the realization that he and Jack were too different. With every page he'd read, that fact became more evident. They'd made him face the truth.

A truth that filled him with shame.

He wasn't strong enough to handle being in this relationship. "Maybe I've been kidding myself thinking that I could do this."

Jack's lips twisted into a frown, and the corners of his eyes turned down. "I heard what you said about my house, but let's start with the books. You didn't like them."

"They scared the crap out of me. All of that violence and terror. And then it ends, and you're not sure whether the good guys really win, and sometimes they don't win at all. It was so… disturbing."

Jack's shoulders sagged, and he drew in on himself. "Let me guess, you're wondering what's wrong with me, right? Like there must be something wrong for me to be able to write that stuff. Hey, you're not the first guy… far from it. But I thought you were different."

The twisting sensation he'd experienced all week returned to Gabe's chest. "I thought I could handle it."

"I don't care if you don't read my books, Gabriel." Jack's voice was weary, and his eyes were sad. "I know a lot of authors whose families or friends don't read their books for whatever reason. It's fine."

"Is it, though? That's your livelihood. I can't be with you and never ask about your work. You love talking about your books. But hearing about it, the ideas, and then reading the words, freaks me out too much." He'd done a lot of things to keep the peace with his family. A lot of compromising on his end because he hadn't wanted to stir the waters and cause a confrontation he wasn't equipped to handle well. He couldn't do that, not with Jack. He couldn't pretend. "You were so excited the other day when you were talking to your readers about books and movies and the horror genre. You lit up. And you really clicked with that guy who asked you out right in front of me."

Jack's eyes narrowed. "I turned him down, didn't I?"

Gabe swallowed hard and gave voice to the words he'd been thinking all week. "Maybe you should have said yes."

"You're kidding, right?"

He dragged a hand through his hair. "We're *so* different. You had a lot more in common with him."

Jack came toward him, hands reaching out, his expression aching and earnest. "I didn't want him. I want you."

"But why? And for how long? How do you know I'm not just your muse for this project?" One by one, his fears tumbled out. He couldn't stop them.

Jack's hands fell to his sides. "That's what you really think?"

"What other reason is there? Once the book is done, and you've moved on to another project, you'll realize you and I have nothing in common." How long would it be before he realized that Gabe wasn't enough? How long before he tossed Gabe to the side without a second thought? The images gutted him. "And how is this going to work long-term? You don't like having your routine messed with. You're usually going to bed right when I'm waking up. And you don't have a problem with disappearing for days on end."

Face red, eyes burning, Jack took a step back. "You're looking for reasons why this can't work."

"No, I'm pointing out problems we've already had. Ones that are real and valid." Gabriel couldn't stop the rush of memories of his brother's comments and sneers. They echoed too loud. Yes, it was the horror stuff that he had a problem with, but it went far deeper than that. He couldn't forget how out of place he felt. How out of place he'd always felt. He'd never fit in Jack's world, and eventually, Jack would realize it too and leave him. "I'm tired of always being the one who has to constantly give in."

"Well, that's your fault." Jack's words snapped out, harsh and angry. "If you don't voice your real opinion on things, how the hell is anyone supposed to know how you really feel? How was I supposed to know how uncomfortable you felt in my house if you never said anything?"

Embarrassment and anger heated him. Jack's words were a direct hit on the thing he hated most about himself, and the thing that was the hardest to change.

Everyone around them was staring.

Gabriel lifted his chin and fought to make his voice steady. "Obviously, this was a mistake. I won't apologize for wanting to make sure that everyone else is comfortable and happy. I don't want to live with a constant struggle of juggling nightmares and pretending everything is fine."

"I don't want to live second-guessing everything I say, have, own, and do, wondering if you're happy with them or are secretly cringing." Jack's wounded gaze would haunt him in his dreams. "I also can't change who I am. I'm sure you'd like it better if I wrote cozy mysteries or cookbooks, but I'm me, scary stories and all."

The words felt like a slap, stinging Gabe down to his core, to the very parts he heated about himself. "I can't change who I am either, though sometimes I wish I could, and I would never ask you to do that. But I don't know where that leaves us."

Jack nodded, expression unreadable. "Neither do I."

Raw and aching, Gabe turned, unseeing, and banged into

Ryan. His friend's hands came up and steadied him. "I need to get out of here."

He was desperate to go home, crawl into bed, and hide out from the world, but he had to work Sebastian's shift at the bakery, the only way he'd been able to get out of playing the game. Not that switching shifts had saved him from an awkward encounter with Jack like he had hoped.

He pushed past Ryan and rushed by his teammates, head down, not making eye contact. The soft grass gave way to hard pavement, and still, he kept up his pace. Getting away as fast as possible was all that mattered.

Things with Jack were finished. Even though he was sure he was doing the right thing, his heart was still ripping into pieces.

CHAPTER THIRTEEN

The doorbell rang, pulling Jack's attention from his computer. One glance at the clock, and he knew who would be behind the door. Same time, every day.

He unfolded his body from his desk, rolling his shoulders and wrists and wincing at the stiffness that had sent in, and went downstairs. When he opened the door, he nodded at Shane. "You might as well just start using your key."

Shifting the bag he held to his other hand, Shane raised a brow. "I would have if you hadn't come down. Come on, let's eat."

Jack closed and locked the door behind Shane, then headed for the kitchen and the coffee maker and started the first cup. No matter how many times he'd told Shane that the daily wellness checks weren't necessary, Shane ignored him. The truth was, they were, and seeing his friend helped.

Shane pulled down mugs, choosing a *Scream* mug for himself and a *Halloween* mug for Jack. "How's it going?"

Every day since the encounter with Gabriel at the softball game, his friend had stopped by with breakfast and asked the same thing, and every day, Jack responded the same way. "Fine."

Miserable. But fine.

Shane pressed the filled mug into Jack's hands. "Sit down. Drink this. Aren't those the same clothes you had on yesterday?"

Jack shuffled toward the table. "You know how I turned my book in a few days ago? My editor just emailed saying it's my best work. They're thrilled."

"That's great."

Jack shrugged. He didn't even care anymore. "I just want that project over. Going through edits again is going to suck." *Tasting Terror* had Gabriel's stamp all over it. Every single reference was like slicing himself open. "And then I'll have to promote it and talk about it for weeks. I'm still getting emails from readers raving about Gabe's cookies."

"Speaking of Gabe." Shane set a breakfast burrito in front of Jack, then unpacked his own meal. Scents of spice and sausage and the sweetness of something still hidden in the bag filled the air.

"Which we aren't." He glared at Shane. He wasn't ready to talk about Gabe. Not yet.

Shane crossed his arms over his chest, brow raised, and chin jutting out, in a stance that brokered no argument. "Which we *are*. It's been two weeks, Jack. You can't hide from the world forever."

"I'm not hiding. You're here every day."

"You haven't been to the gym. You haven't been to family dinner. You haven't been *outside*. You're subsisting on candy and coffee."

He picked up his cup and sipped the dark roasted perfection, but his favorite blend wasn't a comfort or pleasure right now. "Writers are allowed to be eccentric recluses."

Shane's lips twitched. "Okay, I'll give you eccentric, but you're not typically a recluse."

"I'm hurt, all right?" He spoke the words, staring into the cup. Talking about Gabe would be painful, but maybe lancing the wound would help. "Gabe was repulsed by everything about me. I heard him loud and clear. We *all* heard him."

"That's not exactly what he said."

Jack raised his gaze. "The books. My writing. This house. You heard him."

"I did, and again, he didn't say exactly that." With a sigh, Shane sat back, his expression a mixture of sympathy and stubbornness. "Gabe didn't have an easy time growing up. Kind of mirrors what you went through in a way, except that your bullies didn't live at home with you."

Sympathy swelled swiftly, overtaking the aching hurt. No one deserved to go through what Gabe had to endure. His family should have been his biggest supporters. "I know his older brother was awful to him. I think his dad was, too."

"It was bad, and caused a lot of self-esteem issues. I don't think he would've been that upset the other day if he didn't really feel something for you. Deep down, he's scared that he doesn't fit in your life."

"Well, I was scared too. Still am. All the things he pointed out... I'm not used to having to accommodate someone else. I've been shit at it in the past."

Shane regarded him for a long and quiet moment, then said, "For the right person, you'd make the effort."

Now that they were talking about it, he let the thoughts that had been turning over and over in his mind spill out. "Gabe was right about one thing. I do want to be able to discuss my work with someone who really matters to me, and not worry that they're repulsed and wondering what's wrong with me." He pushed his plate away, appetite lost, as it had been for days.

"We all want someone who gets us. Who understands and supports us." Shane's words, wise and soft, pulled Jack's attention back to his friend's face. "You deserve to have that. More than anyone I know, you deserve to be happy. I'd fix everything for you if I could."

Emotions were spiraling too quickly. If he let himself dwell too much on Shane's words, he'd break down. Filing them away to be explored later, he focused back on the concerns about Gabe. "I don't have to drill down deep into plot points with him. I really don't expect him to read my books if he doesn't like the genre. I wasn't lying when I told him that. I wouldn't be offended. But it would be nice to be able to talk about it."

"I think you could do that with him. You did that with *Tasting Terror*, didn't you?"

"A bit, yeah. I didn't go into too many details, but we talked about it."

"Well, there you go."

"And I want to be able to geek out with people over whatever with horror. But Gabe doesn't have to fulfill that role. I'd never expect him to put himself through something he hated. I'd never want him to be unhappy. Hell, I'd be happy just watching baking shows with him, and I could listen to him talk about poetry and romanticism forever."

"You need to talk to him, to tell him all the things you're telling me." Shane pushed Jack's plate into its original spot. "But right now, you need to eat, because when I opened the fridge to grab the creamer, I noticed that you didn't eat the lunch or dinner I left for you yesterday. This is getting to be a bad pattern, Jack."

"I..."

"I get it." Shane's voice gentled even more. "You haven't been hungry. You're not feeling like yourself. You're hurting. But if you faint because your body is in desperate need of fuel and I find you splayed out on the floor like one of the victims in your books, then…"

To satisfy Shane, Jack picked up the burrito and took a bite. Shane had gone out of his way to be a good friend these past few weeks, even more so than usual. Jack owed him so much. He drank more coffee, then looked at Shane. "I told him that I wanted him. Saying those words didn't make a damn bit of difference that day, so why would repeating them matter?"

"If you want him in your life, you need to show him how he'll fit into it, and that you want to make room for him. Like you told me weeks ago, words are meaningless unless they're backed up by actions."

Picking at his burrito, he turned that thought over and over, examining it from every angle. "I can do that, but I need him to want to make room for me too."

"You're right. As my dad would say, it needs to be a two-way street."

He glanced at his friend before turning his attention back to his food. The scars from all the years of being bullied might never fade away, and even though he'd carved out a space for himself, a life he was proud of, that yearning to be celebrated and cherished for who he truly was had never faded. "I… I like who I am now, Shane. I haven't always."

Shane's hand covered his on the table. "I know. You've come a long way from the guy I met back in freshman year. I'm proud of who you are, Jack."

His throat thickened. "You've always stood by me."

"I always will."

"I'm a shit friend compared to you."

"Now you're just talking nonsense."

"Am I? You're the one who calls and texts the most, who makes sure that we see each other. You're the one who—"

Hand raised, Shane shook his head. "I'm going to stop you right there. We've known each other for almost eighteen years. Do you really think I'd still be here if I thought this friendship was one-sided?"

"No. But that doesn't change the fact that I've often been too caught up in what I have going on to pay enough attention to the people around me."

"You've been a good friend, Jack. And you're working on the changes that you promised you'd make." Shane punctuated his statement with his coffee mug. "You're answering calls and texts. You promised not to go radio silent on me, and so far, you haven't. Gabe was a part of why you changed, but don't think for a second that you weren't pulling your weight before."

They ate in silence for a few minutes. Jack replayed Shane's words and simply appreciated that he had Shane in his life. At the moment, there were only so many ways to show that appreciation. Grabbing his friend a refill on the coffee was a start.

Shane accepted his cup with a smile. "So, when are you going to talk to Gabe?"

"If I do try to talk to him, what do I say? That I'm a mess without him? What if he doesn't want me enough to make changes too? What if I can't convince him that my feelings are real and not just based on him being my muse for the book? He'd be better off with some poet who spends his days crafting phrases about love and beauty." His stomach ached at the thought of someone else whispering seductive lines into Gabe's ears.

Sympathy and stubbornness settled into his friend's

features. "I just saw him at the bakery yesterday. He looked as miserable as you. Didn't smile once. Ashley said he's been like that for since your interaction before the softball game."

That wasn't good. Gabriel always had a ready smile for the customers. "I don't want to hurt him more. Do you think it's a mistake for us to try again if he'll have me?"

Shane pushed away his empty plate and sat back in his chair. "Actually, I think you're perfect for each other. You balance each other out. The past month with him is the happiest I've seen you in years. Him, too."

"I don't know how to make him listen."

"You've written your way out of complicated, seemingly impossible scenarios before."

"That's writing, not real life."

"Maybe you can do a combination of the two."

"I don't know…" He lifted his gaze to the ceiling. And then inspiration struck. "Wait. Actually, I *do* know. At least, I hope so. Shane, you're a genius."

Shane shrugged and grinned. "I don't know about that, but it's good to see you smile again."

Energy flowed through his body. He was suddenly starving. Jack hefted the remainder of his burrito. "Let's eat. I have a lot to do if I'm going to try to fix this."

CHAPTER FOURTEEN

"Gabriel?"

"Yeah?" He turned away from washing a mixing bowl and faced his boss. His body ached, and his mind was numb. So numb that he'd mistakenly grabbed salt instead of sugar when baking a special order that morning. It hadn't been his first mistake either. And it wasn't even noon. There were still hours to go in his shift.

"Go home."

His stomach tightened and dropped like a lead weight. "What? Why?"

With a gentle smile and eyes full of concern, Ashley came toward him. "Because you need it."

Sputtering, he dried his hands on his apron. There was a full sink of bowls to be cleaned and icing to be made again, *correctly* this time… "I'm fine. I—"

"You aren't. You haven't been."

His denial died on his lips. Two weeks of mistakes and distracted thoughts were stacked against him.

Two weeks had passed since he and Jack had parted ways. He missed Jack's humor and his hugs, his wit and his kisses, the warmth of his smile, and the heat of his body. Jack happily embraced who he was, something Gabe envied. "I can't leave you and Sebastian. We're so busy."

"Sebastian and I will be fine. I called Xavier. He and Mike are on their way in and will work the front of the shop. And Leo and Kelsey are going to handle deliveries."

Guilt and regret were a potent punch to his gut. He'd caused chaos and extra work for the people who meant the most to him. All because he couldn't shake the heavy weight around his heart. He twisted the apron around his hands so tightly, he nearly snapped the strings around his neck.

The events at the ball field had replayed over and over again in a continuous loop, and had made one thing crystal clear: he'd completely overreacted. He'd thought he'd have more time to formulate his thoughts before he saw Jack. But no. And all of his insecurities had come out in a rush. But maybe it was for the best. Jack deserved to have someone who could share everything with him. Gabe wasn't that person. But he desperately wished that he could be.

"Take the next few days off. I don't want to see you back here until Monday."

Gabriel dragged a hand through his hair and mentally shook himself. He needed to get himself together before he got fired. "I'm sorry, Ashley. I love this job. I don't want to lose it. I'll come back tomorrow, and I promise I'll be better."

"Gabriel." Voice firm, she placed her hands on her hips. "Take the rest of the week off. That's an order. If you come back in before that, I will fire you."

"But, I…" Casting a glance around the room, he searched for a way to convince her.

She smiled again, full of soft sympathy. "A broken heart takes time to heal. This bakery is a family. We all help each other, don't we? Let us help you now. I'll see you on Monday morning."

The pit in his stomach eased but didn't fade. He pulled off his apron and then hung it on the hook by the decorating room's door. "I'll make this up to you."

She patted his shoulder. "Don't worry about anything here, just focus on taking care of yourself."

Guilt and exhaustion and frustration and worry mixed together and settled heavy on his shoulders and in his heart, but he nodded and forced his feet to move toward the door. Voices carrying from the front of the shop announced Mike and Xavier's arrival. Sighing, he stepped into the heat and sunshine.

Ryan waved from his perch on the bench outside the shop. Phone in hand, he stood and pocketed the device. "Hey."

Gabe slowed his steps, suspicious because Ryan never hung outside the back of the shop unless he was visiting Gabe when Gabe was on his lunch break. "What are you doing here?"

"I was with Xavier when Ashley called earlier. I thought I'd walk you home."

He bit back the sigh swelling up from his chest. "I don't need a babysitter."

"But you do need a friend." He gently nudged Gabe with his shoulder. "Come on. Talk to me. I know you didn't want to talk about Jack when the whole thing at the ballfield first happened, and Austin and I respected that, but I think talking now will help."

He fell in step beside his friend, and they walked in silence. After a few blocks, he put voice to the dragging chains slowing his every thought and movement. "I'm tired, Ry."

Ryan's features twisted in sympathy. "Why don't you stay with us for a while? You can have your pick of the guest bedrooms. Everson and I will take care of you."

"I can't do that to you." He couldn't handle being around happy couples right now. They just made him sad. "I'll be okay on my own."

"You haven't been okay. You're a zombie."

They reached his home, and Gabe sat heavily on the front step. He dropped his head into his hands. The ache in his chest encompassed his entire body as though every single cell felt Jack's absence and yearned for him.

Moments from their time together played behind his closed lids as the occasional rumble of a passing car's engine and birds chirping from the trees provided the soundtrack to his internal movie clips.

"Gabe?" Ryan's voice broke into his thoughts, and his knee knocked into Gabe's thigh as Ryan sat beside him.

"I miss him."

"Then call him."

The effort to raise his head seemed monumental, so he didn't. "I can't. He deserves someone who can be everything he needs. I'm not that person."

A shoulder nudge sent Gabe sideways. When he righted himself, glaring at Ryan, his friend simply raised a brow. "Why can't you be his person?"

"You already know why. I don't want to go through it again."

"What I heard that day at the game was a lot of worry and fear. I understand being afraid. Putting yourself out there and being open and vulnerable to someone is scary. Wondering if you can fulfill their needs and if they can fill yours is a huge thing."

Very true. "Jack and I are so different."

"Not on the stuff that really matters. You're both good people. You care about each other. You help each other. You're both good to your friends." Smiling, Ryan lightly touched Gabe's shoulder. The gesture of comfort soothed some of the ache. "I know you better than anyone. And Shane knows Jack. We've watched you two together, listened to you talk about each other. You totally fit."

Having been there when other Brennan siblings were going through dramas and situations that had the whole family weighing in both in their presence and in their absence, he could easily imagine how that conversation had gone down. "Were Jack and I the topic of conversation at the last family dinner?"

"We all care about both of you."

"So, that's a *yes*. Sorry if this is making things weird for you guys."

"It's not." Even if it was, Ryan wouldn't admit it. His friend was too nice.

"Has, um… Have you…" After clearing his throat, he tried again. "How is Jack?"

Ryan shrugged. "I haven't seen him since the game. No one has, except Shane."

He'd hurt Jack that day, and every time he thought about it, fresh pain ripped into his heart. "Did Shane say, is Jack doing okay?"

"From what Shane says, Jack is as miserable as you." Ryan squeezed his shoulder and then pulled him into a brief hug. "Come on, Gabe. Talk to me."

Gabriel exhaled a long expulsion of breath. Maybe talking more would help. Hell, it couldn't make him feel any *worse*, could it? "I want to be what Jack needs. But what if I can't do it? I know my limits, and I tried to push past them, but Ry, I can't deal with the house of horrors. And I'll never be comfortable watching slasher movies or reading gory, disturbing books. I think Jack is brilliant. He should have someone who can be everything he needs."

"What if you're who he needs?"

A bitter laugh escaped him. "How can I be? I just gave you the reasons that I'm not."

"You've cooked for him, made sure he had food in his fridge, baked for him, supported him at his book signing, made him feel better about playing softball with us. You've made him happier."

"I don't know… None of those things were that big, were they?"

"I think, deep down, you're worried that Jack won't believe that you're someone worth fighting for." Ryan's quiet words stunned him. "I've heard your stories about your family. I've been in the same room with you when you've called them. I've seen you with your brother. I know how your dad and brother make you feel. Your family did a number on your self-esteem and confidence. But Gabe, you are worth fighting for. You're strong, and smart, and creative, and one of the best friends anyone could ask for. Hell, you're like my brother. I love you. My family loves you. You're worthy of friendship and love. You need to believe it."

The backs of his eyes pricked with tears. He viciously blinked, but the sting of prisms still washed into his gaze. He focused on a spot on the sidewalk and fought hard to battle for control.

Ryan's hand, gentle and supportive on his shoulder, broke him. "Look at me. You're worth it, Gabriel."

One look into Ryan's blue eyes, sympathetic and earnest and sad, and the dam burst. Tears rolled hot down his cheeks, his shoulders shook, and he couldn't catch his breath or force words through his thickened throat.

Ryan's arms came around him, and Gabe hung on. Bitterness and loneliness and anger and fear swept over him in overlapping waves as memories of ruined birthdays and holidays and stolen bicycles and destroyed books and all of the taunts and insults he'd heard over the years tumbled to the surface, shining light on parts of himself that he needed to heal.

Finally, the storm subsided. Worn out, Gabe raised his head. Embarrassment threatened to engulf him. "Ry…"

"Don't." Ryan silenced his worry with another squeeze before letting go. "This is me, remember? Safe space, here. You needed to let that out."

He nodded because Ryan was right. "Thanks for being there for me. If we're being honest, for a long time, I thought you and your family were too good to be true. But then I started thinking that you were my second chance, you know? The brothers I never had. The family I always wanted."

"You're stuck with us now. They've all adopted you."

"Are you really okay with that?" He'd never dared ask that question before.

"Are you kidding?" Ryan wrapped an arm around his shoulders once again. "I know I'm lucky to have the family that I do. I'm more than happy to share them with you, Gabe. You're as important to us, too, you know. If you need more proof, we can call each of them right now. They'll tell you the same thing."

His emotions were running too high and too raw for more conversations. Besides, he'd experienced the warmth, love, and acceptance multiple times over the past few years. "I believe you."

"Now that's cleared up, back to Jack. What do you want to do?"

He took a deep breath, sat with his feelings, and there was only one answer written on his heart. "I want him."

"If you want to, you can find a way. Just like the saying."

Doubt crept in, hooking its claws into the edges of his hope. "Trouble is, we both would need to want to. What if Jack doesn't?"

The confidence in Ryan's gaze restored Gabe's resolve. "Then, Austin and I will invade your house, take awesome care of you, and help you pick up the pieces."

They would. No matter what happened, he would have people around him. People who loved him just as he was, exactly as he was. Hopefully, Jack would feel that way about him too. "Let me go inside and get cleaned up. Then I'll go talk to him."

But before he laid his heart on the line, there was another stop he had to make first.

After a shower, a snack, and a trip to the store, Gabriel headed over to Jack's house, clutching the small paper bag that held a small token of his commitment to Jack. He was ready to talk... if Jack would hear him out.

At Jack's door, he glanced at his reflection in the beveled glass and ran a hand over his shirt. It was the same one he'd worn when Jack had visited him after his birthday.

Steeling himself, he knocked.

After a few seconds, movement reflected through the glass. The lock clicked, the door opened, and Jack stood before him as handsome as ever, freshly shaved, hair tamed, and dressed in dark gray shorts and a black T-shirt that looked brand new. His brows rose, and his mouth dropped open as he scanned Gabe in a quick once over. "You're here."

"Is this a bad time? Are you going out?" He didn't want to think about Jack on his way to meet someone else.

Jack pushed the door open wide and gestured for Gabriel to come inside. "I was actually on my way to see you."

The words eased the lead weight in his stomach. If Jack were coming to see him, that had to be good, right? He hurried in. Then stopped and stared as the sound of the door closing echoed behind him. The living room was completely devoid of everything scary. "What happened? Did you get robbed by a horror movie buff or something?"

"I moved the things I wanted to keep into my office and donated the rest. I want you to feel comfortable when you're here. That is if you're going to be here." He stood by the door, biting his lip, dark eyes darting from Gabe to the floor and back again.

"You did all of that for me?" Gabriel gaped at him as warmth expanded in his chest. "Jack, I don't want you to change who you are."

"I'm not. Not really. But some things are more important, some *people* are more important, and I want to show you that." Two steps forward, and Jack hesitated again, lifting his hands before he shoved them into his pockets. "I got some new coffee mugs too. Light blue, like the ones at your place. And a new shower curtain. New towels and kitchen stuff, too, and nothing scary is hanging in the hallway anymore. Basically, all of the horror is confined to one room. And I'm now on a sleep schedule that's more compatible with yours, in bed by midnight and up by seven. Well, that part is a work in progress, but I'm hoping to be on a somewhat more compatible schedules with you."

Air left Gabe's lungs. His heart seemed to freeze for a moment. He fought to drag in a breath as a tingle worked its way through his blood. Surprise and hope shot through him like sunbeams streaming through clouds. "I don't know what to say."

A smile tugged at Jack's cheeks. "I also promise to keep my phone on and actually look at it at least once a day, no matter what else is going on, writing or not, and respond back to messages right away. I need to be better at showing the people in my life that I care about them."

Gabriel moved closer. Jack had made compromises for him. It was time to be just as brave. He pushed his shoulders back and set his jaw. He could do this. "I apologize for the way I overreacted that day at the ball field. I was upset, and all of my insecurities came out. You're amazing and deserve to be with someone who can be everything you need. I wasn't sure if I could be that person for you."

Brown eyes widened. "You are—"

"But I want to be. More than anything." Holding onto hope, he handed Jack the small paper bag. "I brought you something new for your collection."

Jack opened it and spilled the contents onto his palm, grinning at the set of tiny figurines of classic horror movie icons. "Thank you. I can't believe you bought this."

"It's a small start. I got the audio versions of your books too. Hearing your voice narrating them…" His voice broke as memories of those lonely days flooded him. "I wasn't sure if I'd screwed this up too much, and that would be the only way I'd hear your voice again."

Jack set the gift aside and reached for Gabe's hand. After a moment's hesitation, he grabbed hold and gently squeezed. "I meant it when I said it's okay if you don't read my books. Or listen to them. As long as you don't walk away from me…"

"I don't want to walk away." He tightened his hold, soaking up the warmth and reveling in the sensation of having Jack's hand in his once again. "I'll be honest, I had to skip ahead when things got too gory."

"Which is fine." Voice firm, Jack drew him closer until his other arm wrapped around Gabriel's waist, and they stood torso to torso. "You know your limits. Gore isn't your thing. I wouldn't expect you to read or listen to something that upsets you or you don't care for. You sure my books didn't turn you off me, though?"

Smiling, Gabe shook his head and brought their joined hands up to rest on his chest. "What you said that day, that people think something is wrong with you because you write that stuff? I don't think anything's wrong with you. You're imaginative and creative. I'm fascinated by the way your mind works. As much as I got freaked out, I don't think that would have happened if you weren't such a talented writer. You're brilliant."

Brows raised, Jack gaped at him, surprise and disbelief and joy spanning across his features. "Really?"

"I was scared you'd leave me because we're so different, and you'd realize someday that I'm not what you need. I thought I was doing the right thing by stepping back, but I missed you so much my heart hurt. I don't want to lose you." He glanced at their fingers laced together. A perfect fit.

"I don't want to lose you either. I can't guarantee that I'll get everything right, but I promise to try."

"Me too. I can't say I'll watch every horror movie with you, but I wouldn't mind sitting with you while you watch them. I can cuddle next to you, with earbuds in and read a book. And maybe I could try watching a few. I think it would help if you add commentary, and talk about why you like things so much. You light up when you're excited about things. It's beautiful."

Jack brought their joined hands to his lips and kissed

Gabe's knuckles. "I'd like that. Then afterward, we can watch a baking show or something else that's happy to take your mind off of it. Of course, I'm happy to distract you in other, more intimate ways."

They shared a smile, and Gabriel traced his finger along the side of Jack's face. "I want you to talk to me about your books too. What you do is a part of you, and I want to share everything. Maybe not the gory details, but I can handle broader story arcs."

Smile wide and eyes sparkling, Jack pulled him closer, tightening his hold. "Thank you. That means a lot to me. Speaking of writing, I have something for you."

"Is it the finished manuscript? Ryan said that you turned it in to your editor, and they loved it."

Keeping their hands joined, Jack drew him further into the room and picked up a small leather-bound book from the coffee table. "They did, but this is something else. Something no one has seen. This is the journal I kept when writing *Tasting Terror*. It has all of my notes about plot ideas and what I learned in the bakery. But more than anything, it's about you. It has everything I learned about you and how you made me feel. I hope it will show you how serious I am about giving us a chance."

Hands trembling, Gabriel took the book and opened to the first page and read the first line. *I saw Gabriel today, and suddenly everything clicked into place.*

Tears pricked his eyes as he read the detailed account of their first softball game, and then Jack's notes on his impressions from meeting Gabe at their friends' events. Page after page of their time together from that first softball game up to the last one, and then the days after when Jack was alone, editing his book, sad and missing him. Line after line of Jack talking about things he loved about Gabriel.

Loved.

He'd actually used that word.

Gabriel closed the book and blinked away the prisms clouding his vision. "This is my most favorite book of all time."

"Yeah?" With a watery laugh, Jack tugged a hand through his curls. His eyes were wet too. "It's yours to keep if you want it."

"I do." He carefully set the book on the coffee table and swallowed around the lump in his throat. "I'm falling in love with you, Jack. I want so many things, so many experiences with you. I came here today hoping to convince you to give me another shot, but I never imagined all of this would happen."

Jack encircled Gabriel in his embrace. "I'm falling in love with you too. You and me, we're good together. I like who I am with you. I like who we are together."

Warmth and pleasure spun out, radiating through him. Gabriel sought out Jack's lips. The kiss was a promise, filled with hopes and dreams and wishes. "I do, too. And I can't wait to see what the next chapter holds."

CHAPTER FIFTEEN

Jack rubbed his hands over his face and then stared at the scene filling his laptop screen. No doubt about it, this was the coolest thing he'd ever written. The screenplay for *Tasting Terror* was complete.

Seeing the novel that had brought Gabe and him together come to life on the big screen would be amazing.

He stood and stretched and smiled at the photo of Gabriel and himself that he kept on his desk, taken at the Halloween party they'd hosted together when Jack's home had been filled with people from the softball team, the gym, the bakery, and the Brennan family. The photo captured them smiling at each other, wrapped in each other's arms. Out of everything in his office, all the memorabilia, the framed covers of his books, that photo was his most favorite thing in the room.

Time to find the man who was his most favorite person in the world.

Sounds and scents drifting from the kitchen meant Gabriel was baking. He headed down the stairs and through a house that was looking more like bits of Gabriel and him blended together every day. He wanted more of that. More of everything.

Gabriel looked up from contemplating a tray of cupcakes. Flour dusted his sweater, and smears of frosting dotted his forearms. His face lightened into a smile. "Are you done for the day?"

"Yeah. And not only that, but I got all the way to the end of the screenplay. It's finished." Jack leaned in for a kiss and then lingered at the delicious feel of Gabriel's soft lips. "How about you? What are you baking?"

"I know the movie premiere will be a long way off, but you'll need a cake for it, so I started thinking of flavors. This is a dark chocolate cupcake with cream cheese frosting and a strawberry compote center. I have other ideas for flavors based on certain scenes. And I marked off ideas for things we can add to the cake for decoration." He patted his auto-graphed copy of *Tasting Terror*. Dozens of yellow and blue sticky notes stuck out of the sides. "And yes, I am aware that it's really early to be thinking about the premiere when you've only just finished the screenplay, but I'm just so proud and excited for you."

Jack grinned. Gabriel had come a long way.

They both had.

In the seven months since they'd been together, they'd slept over each other's places at least four nights a week, were together as often as time allowed, and had fallen into the deepest intimacy he'd ever felt with another human being. It wasn't all smooth sailing. He occasionally got frustrated when people and plans interrupted his work, and Gabriel occasionally slipped back into the habit of not voicing his preferences and opinions, but they worked through the bumps and were stronger for it.

Damn, he was a lucky man.

Holding Gabriel's endlessly blue gaze, Jack wrapped his arms around his boyfriend's waist. "That's really sweet. I love that you want to make a cake for it. We can go with whatever you think is best. Pick your favorite part."

"You know my favorite part. The book's dedication. *For Gabriel. With Love*." The sweetest smile bloomed on his face, and Gabriel nuzzled his cheek.

The four words were simple, but to Jack, they meant so much more. They were a promise. He'd do anything for the man who held his heart. Anything at all.

Gabriel swiped his finger through a bit of leftover frosting and held it to Jack's lips. His eyes closed when Jack drew the digit into his mouth.

Jack lapped at the sweetness and then nipped the pad. At Gabriel's soft groan, he released his hold and then edged closer, desperate to feel Gabe's lips against his own. The kiss fused them together, lips to lips and heart to heart as they eliminated all space between them. On a groan, Jack changed the angle and deepened the kiss. As always, Gabriel tasted sweet. Like sugar and chocolate and the promise of happily ever after.

With a sigh, Gabe lifted his head and then brushed his thumb along Jack's cheek. "Come upstairs. I need to shower. I'm covered in flour, and you have frosting on your face and flour on your shirt."

A glance at his shirt confirmed the damage. "What time do we need to be at Ryan's for dinner?"

"We should leave in about an hour. It'll be a full house. All of the Brennans are going to be there, and Sebastian and Austin are coming too. I think I'll bring the cupcakes with us, and they can taste test for me."

"Good idea." Heart full, Jack drew him into another kiss. "I love you, Gabriel."

Gabriel's gaze grew soft. "I love you too, Jack."

"Move in with me." The words spilled out, startling him. This wasn't how he'd intended to bring up the idea of living together.

Given Gabriel's raised brows and open mouth, he was just as surprised. But then his eyes gleamed, and his hands slid around Jack's shoulders, keeping him close.

"You mean it?" Gentle strokes accompanied Gabriel's words. "You're ready?"

Leaning into the capable hands, Jack nodded. "Are you?"

"So ready. The last seven months have been the happiest of my life. I want more."

The love for the man standing in the circle of his arms beat with a fierceness that was all-consuming. "Every day with you, I'm reminded of how lucky I am to have you. Let's go upstairs so I can show you how much you mean to me."

Hand in hand, they walked through the house. Jack could picture where Gabriel's things would fit, how things could be arranged to make his space fully theirs.

They reached the bedroom. Wrapped around each other, exchanging lingering kisses and caresses, they couldn't get close enough fast enough. When they turned toward the bed, Jack smiled at the sight of the rumpled sheets and blankets from a rare lazy morning spent reading together. With Gabriel moving in, they'd have a lot more chances for mornings just like that one.

He glanced at the bedside clock as Gabriel drew him onto the soft sheets. They needed to get ready to join their friends. And soon. But first, they needed to bask in the sunshine of starting their own happy ending.

Thank you for reading Gabe and Jack's story! If you enjoyed the story, I would greatly appreciate if you could please leave a review. Reviews, even one line long, help other readers find my books.

Want more of the Brennans? Check out Ryan and Everson's romance in MAD SCRAMBLE.

Everson Montgomery's entire life is devoted to ensuring the success of his pro football career. Strict rules about his diet, sleep habits, and training schedule keep him running like a well-oiled linebacker machine. There's zero room for distractions… until he meets his teammate's brother and is instantly smitten with the friendly, gorgeous, generous man.

Ryan Brennan has had a crush on the gridiron giant for years. When the opportunity to work together on a charity drive arises, he's all in. Spending time with Everson, he sees the sweetness and vulnerability beneath the stoic exterior, and opens up his heart and his home. He's learned the hard way that getting too close, too fast isn't smart, but something keeps drawing him to Everson.

Everson doesn't do relationships and Ryan doesn't do hook ups, but they can't stay away from each other. When chaos on the field and in the locker room spills over into everyday life, and past ghosts return to haunt them both, will they chase after their hearts or will their relationship be tackled before they have a chance to score?

Visit https://susanscottshelly.com/books

ABOUT THE AUTHOR

USA TODAY bestselling author Susan Scott Shelley writes romances with heat and heart that celebrate love without limits. Enormous mugs of coffee and tea make her happy, as does reading romance novels and binging episodes of her favorite British TV shows. Susan also works as a professional voiceover artist, and while she's definitely a city girl, she likes being out in nature as often as possible. A fan of mythology, word games, and hockey, she lives in Philadelphia with her husband and has yet to meet a plant she hasn't wanted to take home.

Learn more at http://www.susanscottshelley.com.

ALSO BY SUSAN SCOTT SHELLEY

The Philadelphia Power series

Against the Rush, Over the Top

Love & Rugby: Season of Love

Savor, Seduce, Stay

Love & Rugby series

Spiral, Spark, Smolder, Shine, Surprise, Swoon

The Falling series

Falling Faster, Falling Harder, Falling Slowly

Bliss Bakery series

Sugar Crush, Sweet Hearts

The Buffalo Bedlam series

Making His Move, Fighting For More, Taking His Shot

Skating On Chance, Holding On Tight, Scoring Slater

Playing to Win, vol.1 (books 1-3), Playing to Win, vol.2 (books 4-6)

The Philadelphia Frenzy series

Mad Scramble, Hometown Hero

Holiday Hearts series

Kiss Me Again, More Than Words, All I Want, Marry Me, Holiday
Hearts (series collection)

Rocked by Love series

Love Notes, Love Song

Game of Love series

Rekindled, Captivated, Enamored,

Game of Love (series collection)

Stay up-to-date with Susan via her newsletter:

http://www.susanscottshelley.com/newsletter.

www.ingramcontent.com/pod-product-compliance
Lightning Source LLC
Chambersburg PA
CBHW060945180626
46817CB00004B/1711